A Prince of Earth

(BOOK 2 OF THE HISTORIES OF EARTH)

A PRINCE
OF EARTH

A NOVEL BY STEVEN J. CARROLL

-GLOBE LIGHT PRESS-
FOREST FALLS, CA

A Prince of Earth
Globe Light Press :

Globe Light Press

Globe Light Press
Printed in the United States of America

For questions regarding large or bulk orders of this book
please address: Globe Light Press, Globelightpress@gmail.com

Connect with other Prince of Earth fans:
facebook.com/stevenjcarrollauthor
www.stevenjcarroll.com

For all the honor we have yet to earn.

ACKNOWLEDGEMENTS

A great big thanks to Laurenish Designs, for her wonderful interior title. Thanks to Christine Hysell for her excellent work as an editor, and to Chad Lewis for his extraordinary cover art.

And my best thanks to my wife, Bre. You are my greatest ally and friend.

FOREWORD

There is a story, once told, about a young girl named Delany Calbefur, and of her fantastical journeys outside of our world and into another. Into the realm of Gleomu, to be precise, on a planet very far from our own, and she came to that place at what would seem to be the exact right time, saving a prince and his kingdom from ever certain destruction.

However, indeed, that was a very long time ago, and the true memory of this brave girl has all but faded from our world, though not entirely. The tales of her adventures being first recorded in a book which I have called *In the Window Room*, and which should be read before continuing this story, or else nothing that should happen hereafter will make any sense.

CHAPTER ONE
THE COUNTRYSIDE

T he greens of the countryside passed by at a blurry pace. The make and pedigree of his family's car made for a smooth ride, yet Timothy Hayfield still felt sick to his stomach.

"Wipe that sour expression off your face at once," ordered his mother, glaring intently at him through the reflection in the driver's mirror.

Timothy looked up from his lonely spot in the backseat, up toward his mother who was cleverly dressed for the occasion, and fitted in a fanciful summer's hat, but he would not change his appearance for her sake.

"You're going to visit your grandmother. You're not dying," she continued.

But it felt like he was dying, or at least partially. To waste away a whole good summer, stuck with his ailing grandmother in Mayfield, while all his schoolmates and friends had splendid holidays planned at beach cottages, or in getaways to the city, all this did make Timothy feel as if he were dying, or at least made him hope to.

The car eased to turn off the main road. Under the tires, cracks in the pavement became noticeably more pronounced. Till unexpectedly, with a loud thump, a rather large dip caught him by surprise, jolting his hand that rested beneath his chin, causing him to inadvertently wallop himself in the jaw.

"Ouch," he cried, his cheek throbbing. The right side of his face now smarting awfully bad, he rubbed his chin vehemently, feeling sorrier for himself as he did.

"What's the matter now?" his mother asked, seeming to have become exhausted by his protests, so that she did not show the same sort of care he'd been used to.

"Nothing," he said, still trying to rub the ache from his cheekbone. "Nothing at all," he whispered, but only to himself, thinking this pain to be a remarkably appropriate way to begin such a lurid summer's holiday.

The car drove on.

After a passing minute they came to a fork in the road, and a carved stone sign directing the way to the "Mayfield School for Girls". Why his grandmother should choose to make a residence for herself on the grounds of such a snooty old boarding school was beyond his understanding.

"*Such a terribly boring place,*" he thought, as their car ebbed to a stop in front of a closed black iron gate.

"Who are you here for, madam?" asked the watchman, in a grey and black chauffeur's cap.

"Matilde Wolcott, please," his mother replied.

CHAPTER TWO
MATILDE WOLCOTT
✦

Matilde Wolcott, Timothy's grandmother, who in her younger years had gone by the name Mattie Hardy, now lived alone in a large antique, but handsomely renovated old home on the grounds of the Mayfield School for Girls, where Matilde, herself, had been a pupil.

And here is a short history of how she came to such a residence (and I shall try my best to be brief, but bear it in mind, that to condense the wealth of someone's life down to only a few pages is no small task. Especially if they'd made for themselves such a full life, as Matilde had):

After graduating with high marks from Mayfield, Mattie decided to make a career for herself, and was very fond of writing (and of journalism, in particular). And so, at the direction of her parents, and with little effort on her part, she applied and was accepted into a prestigious girl's college in the Americas, in Boston.

There she met, and fell in love with, an upstanding gentleman, well liked by his peers, a loveable graduate medical student with a family history in the profession. And six months later, they were married and Mattie Hardy became Mrs. Wilbur Charles Douglas Wolcott, II. (On a lesser note, it is good practice to never fault someone for their birth name, being that it is always of far greater importance how men speak of you, than the name by which you are addressed.)

After this, Matilde and Wilbur decided to stay in Massachusetts, making a small, but lovely, home for themselves near Cape Cod. During this time, she was awarded a position at the Boston Globe, where she quickly excelled as an editor and a columnist.

They had three children, who in order by age were: Martin, Agatha (Timothy's mother), and Matthew. Their oldest, Martin, flew for America in the war, and was shot down during a bombing raid on a German supply station, on March 16th, 1945. And for his sacrifice, and for theirs, Matilde and Wilbur were offered a wrapped and folded, starred and striped flag, and a purple heart for valor, both of which she still keeps in a display case on the mantle, but from that day onward she found it extremely unbearable to fly in a plane, and would do so only out of absolute necessity.

And when the war had at last ended, the Wolcott's moved back to England, with their adolescent children, so that Matilde might be nearer to her parents, and to help them rebuild their lives after the destructive conflict that had left them frail and nearly destitute, after so many years.

But in so doing, there was only one house that Mattie wished to buy, to settle in with her young family, and no other place would have ever been good enough. That

5

house being an old grey, two story manor on the grounds of Mayfield. Which, at the time, was in dire need of repair (and what Wilbur thought to be a very poor investment, as houses go, though he was kind enough not to make too much fuss over it, or at least no more than he should). But as he soon came to realize, that mysterious ill kept estate was the only home Matilde wanted, and rightly so.

Thud, Thud, Thud.

Agatha used the heavy, lion headed knocker to strike at the face of the door. The sound of it reverberated through the emptiness of that grey house.

But there was no answer.

Heaped up at Timothy's knees was a large packed bag, filled to overflowing, with all the many sorts of things he had thought to have needed, to last him throughout the length of such a presumably unentertaining holiday.

"That's odd," Agatha muttered, going past Timothy and leaning over the porch railing to check again for her mother's car, and seeing it to be right where she had last imagined it.

"Does that mean I don't have to stay?" Timothy asked, thinking maybe he'd had a turn of good fortune, after all.

But to this his mother turned and pointed at him harshly, so that he knew he would not be so lucky, and that he daren't make another mention of forgoing his summer duties.

"Hello?" Agatha said like a question, turning the brass handle of the door open with a creak, and peering her head inside. Yet there was still no response.

And leaving his vastly oversized luggage at the landing of the staircase, Timothy was led on a search throughout that vacant mansion-like home.

To his reliable memory, this was the first real time he'd ever come to visit his grandmother at Mayfield. The only other time before then, being while he was still quite young, and his only memory of that, just a vague image of himself seated on his grandfather's lap, eating chocolates. However, this was such a wide marvelous place, that Timothy would have liked to have kept a memory of it: with rooms filled with tapestries and odd figurines, and suits of full armor (most grown-up sized and human like, but some at odd proportions with longer thinner waists, or with shorter stockier legs than would be normal).

"Hello? You here, mum?" Agatha would call out intermittently, but they never heard a reply, not even the faintest whisper. The entire house seemed bone dry of any living thing.

When, at last, they had prodded through every other portion of that lofty house that Timothy's mother knew to look through, they came finally to the end of a hall, and a closed attic door. Which was instantly peculiar, seeing as every other bedroom door or study had been left opened.

"You mustn't ever try this yourself," Timothy's mother mentioned. "Grandmother simply abhors people going into her private study." Then a shade quieter, she added, "Grandfather was the only one she'd ever let in with her."

And with that, she plucked up her determination and tried at the knob, but found it to be locked and bolted from the inside.

Then, appearing from thin air, as if from nowhere and all of a sudden, there was a muddled high-pitched mechanical sound, one that Timothy found hard to describe, and a faint, but apparent, flash of white light from beneath the door jam.

"Mother, are you alright?" Agatha asked.

From inside the room, they heard frantic shuffling noises, and the sound of something being dragged across the floorboards.

"Who is it?" Timothy heard an elderly woman's voice at last, echoing from across the locked room.

"It's me... Agatha, mother," she yelled back through the shut door.

"You're early," the woman's voice answered.

"Not anymore," he heard his mother say to herself. Then aloud, "Didn't you get my message? I managed an earlier flight into La Guardia, to make it in time for Thomas's performance."

The door quickly unbolted, and was flung open in a flash. And there, standing before him, to his amazement, was his grandmother, Matilde Wolcott, elaborately adorned in a pale ivy green, fifteenth century style dress, with tiny white flowers woven through her grey and brown streaked hair.

The sight of which wholly shocked Timothy, though his mother seemed to be accustomed to such a show.

"What are you wearing?" she said, folding her arms across her own pleated blouse.

"Oh, can't a girl dress up to see her only British grandson?" his grandmother answered, fluttering down to kiss both his cheeks firmly.

"And you know I can't work that confounded answering contraption you'd got for me," she continued, directing her attention to Agatha now.

"It's called an answering machine, mother, and how am I ever to get a hold of you, then?" Timothy's mother replied, shortly, but sounding lovingly pestered.

"Well, I suppose, you'll just have to call me when I'm at home, won't you?" Matilde answered, grabbing Agatha by the shoulders, and puckering a large kiss onto her cheek as well.

To my best knowledge, it was right at this moment that Timothy Hayfield was forced to change his mind regarding his proposed summer's holiday in Mayfield. Thinking to himself, that whatever his time here may turn out to be, it should most certainly not be boring.

CHAPTER THREE
THE FIRST-YEARER
✦

B arbara Cholley did not like being called names: not a coward, not a chicken, nor any other name that the reprehensible Victoria Delflower wished to call her.

The sun in the noonday sky had grown heated, and had begun to redden Barbara's cheeks. As she stood near the fountain in the courtyard, arms folded, feeling like her skin was about to boil.

"I am not," Barbara blurted out.

"You are too," was Victoria's response. "Only cowards won't go out and touch the door... We've *all* done it."

And Barbara looked around at the gathering crowd of girls that surrounded her during the last few minutes of lunch hour at Mayfield, on a thursday, the last full day of Spring Term.

She had hoped to have avoided such a mess like this, pouring over her studies ever since she'd first arrived at Mayfield last fall, but as it appeared now, in the end, all she'd had to show for her efforts were exemplary scores in geometry. She had not managed, however, to sneak past her duty as a "first-yearer," like she had hoped.

"No use fighting, you know you have to," one of the girls from the crowd said aloud, who appeared to be trying to make the process easiest for all involved.

But Barbara wouldn't budge.

"Why? Sara Darby hasn't," she said, although knowing this to be an uncalled for blow at somewhat of a new friend.

"Oh, come on," yelled one of the tall girls from the back of the group, a girl who had just so happened to be Sara's bunkmate. "You know she got as far as she could... till she saw the flash of light from the gable window, like we all did. She came running back here, crying, and vomited in the common loo."

And Barbara knew she was wrong to have tried to use the little Darby girl's misfortunes, and weak stomach, to her own advantage.

"Do you really want her to have a go at it, again?" the tall girl continued.

"No," Barbara sighed. And then muttered, "It's just not fair, is all I'm saying..." Though she was quick to see that her last words had gone a step too far, by all the nasty glares she'd soon received.

Then Victoria spoke aloud to the group, as if she had wanted to settle the issue once and for all, and like she were an unelected leader of sorts. "So... what'll it be, Cholley?" she asked with a gleam in her eye. "You going for it tonight, or will you be a coward for the rest of your life?"

The fifteen or so girls who had joined around that early afternoon to see what would happen fell instantly, and morbidly quiet. They all stood in shocked amazement. And what is worse, Barbara's anger at such a mean spirited snipe, as Victoria Delflower was, seemed to cloud her good senses.

So that she could not manage to stop herself from saying it.

"Fine, fine... I'll do it," Barbara said, sounding exasperated.

At her surrendering, some in the crowd let out small cheers, that the matter was finally over, yet some were honestly proud of Barbara for finally going through with it.

But even their simple half-hearted congratulations caused a sneer to go across Victoria's face.

"You may go touch the door, but you're still a coward," she said, like she couldn't stand the thought of anyone other than herself being cheered for.

And turning to walk away, Victoria was suddenly stopped cold in her tracks. When Barbara issued out these words, words that she has never known quite why she had said, but thinking they could be blamed, mostly on her present anger at the vicious girl who'd been chiding her for so long.

Speaking out with her head raised, she said, as bravely as she could, "I'll even go inside."

And then gulping her breath in, for she knew she was mad to continue, "All the way up to the attic gable."

The entire crowd around the courtyard fountain lay riddled with silence. Barbara's tongue felt bitter cold, like icicles.

"How could I have been so foolish?" she thought to herself.

It was murder to step inside Wolcott Manor, so much so that no one had ever done it, let alone to try to sneak up to the gable, by one's self, alone in the dark. It was absolute murder.

CHAPTER FOUR

MURDER

✦

"Ah, you've killed me again," Timothy exclaimed, looking over the octagon shaped, chess-like board in front of him, desperately trying to retrace his movements to discover how he had been beaten, so handily.

"Yes, but you're getting better," Matilde said smiling, like maybe she was just being a good sport to encourage her grandson.

"Hardly," he let out, and went back again to examining the game board before him.

The two had passed the time that night engaged in several long spirited rounds of "Ether-rian", as his grandmother called it. Which was the most bizarre variation of chess that Timothy could've imagined, with pieces for giants and dragons, and actual troop movements (like you might find on one of those large maps that generals use to plan wars).

The pair had been playing intently since well before sunset, and by then it was nearing midnight, as Matilde began to disassemble the game pieces, placing them into a clever, gold-lined box.

"Can we play again tomorrow night?" Timothy asked, as his grandmother removed the final knight piece from the board.

"My dear, you are a sore loser, aren't you?" she smiled at him. Which was a true statement, although Timothy didn't like to think of himself in those terms.

"Nooo," he held out the word to emphasize it. "I just want to figure this out," he said, placing his forehead on his hands (like you might do if you've been frustrated), and knowing that he'd been royally beaten that night.

Matilde gave her grandson a tender look.

Then she smirked, and patted him lovingly on the cheek. "Fine, I'd be happy to let you lose again, if you'd like."

"Now off to bed with you," she continued, ushering him away from the kitchen table and through the hallway, toward his downstairs bedroom.

His head was tired from over thinking. He skidded his feet on the wood floor planks, and he thought to expect, as we all might, a restful night's sleep in his new feathery bed. But certainly, things do not always go as planned. For tonight was, indeed, intended to be a tad bit more than restful.

Barbara did wish that the girls on her floor would not have been so tearful in their goodbyes, as she crept carefully from the wing of her dormitory, on the final night of the school year. Being shrouded by the dim light of a new moon, she made it out across the field and along the dirt path that led to the Wolcott house, a pale dusty grey by the low starlight, like a tombstone set on a hill.

"Could the legends be true?" she thought, as she edged toward that beastly house, feeling in no rush to come to her fate. Could Matilde Wolcott really have killed her best friend and hid the evidence of her murder in that distant attic gable?

It seemed an unlikely thing to believe in, but then again, how could every girl at Mayfield be wrong about such a thing. And considering, if it were true, how she would likely be in such dire and immediate danger.

The tip of her quarter-high shoe clipped the brim of a large rock, hidden along the path by the shadows and blackness of that night. She nearly fell.

Surely, weighing her options, running back now washed in fake tears might be acceptable. And then, perhaps forcing herself to vomit in the common loo would be a better fate than this.

However, Barbara Cholley was not as cowardly as all that, and did not prefer to be called names. And so she trudged onward, toward the unlit victorian home on the crest of the hill overlooking Mayfield, knowing that whatever happened now would be unavoidable; Thinking that a brave death at the hands of that "wicked old hag," Matilde Wolcott (as she was poorly called by some of the girls Barbara had grown acquainted with), that it would be a better fate than cowardice.

And in so doing she came to the malevolent front porch steps of that sinister looking house, in the deep darkness of that night, and took in a sizable breath. "Ready?" she asked herself, breathing out.

CHAPTER FIVE

THE BURGLAR

H is room and the rest of that grand house was by now completely darkened.

Timothy had been drifting on the edges of sleep for sometime that evening, and was almost entirely dreaming when he'd heard a sound. But not just any sound, this one being a faint high-pitched coo. Of the kind that a young girl might make, if she had been lurking through an unfamiliar home in the middle of the night, and had accidentally kicked a heavy, and altogether ill placed, decorative statue.

(Which incidentally was exactly what had happened to Barbara that night, and what had caused her to give a highly restrained yelp of pain. One that was just loud enough, however, to be heard from the main floor, and by Timothy, who was not yet fast asleep.)

His eyes opened fully, a bit scared. He stirred on his mattress, grasping at the bed comforter, hoping that quite possibly he had only imagined that sound. Yet still, to be safe, he listened intently at the chance that there might indeed be an intruder fumbling around in his grandmother's large home, a home that was intriguing by the daylight hours, but still, altogether eerie to him after nightfall.

Goose pimples ran up the back of his neck. He had heard another tiny noise, what could possibly be the telltale creaking of an old wooden stair. It was obvious now, a burglar had got into the house.

(At this present time, you must bear in mind, that Timothy had not the luxury of history, as you and I now have, having no means at all by which to understand that these present sounds were being made by an innocent and terribly frightened young girl. And seeing as, while even in the midst of false dangers men may show true bravery, Timothy Hayfield did a very brave thing indeed, if not entirely thought out.)

Springing from beneath his covers, he swiped at the base of a silvery candlestick that had been set upon a small bedroom table near his door. And sneaking in his house slippers quietly through the downstairs hall, being sure to lift the candlestick holder high up in the air above his shoulder, to be used as a ready weapon like one might hold a sword or an American baseball bat, he tip-toed down the unlit hallway.

His breaths were shallow. His footsteps lightly chosen. He reached the bottom of the staircase and saw the vague shadow of an outline, which turned left at the top of the stairs and vanished from his sight. Although it was still remarkably dark, and by that time nearly impossible to know with any certainty the size of the figure, or to whom that shadow had belonged.

He snuck cautiously up the stairs, his steps being cushioned by his well padded evening slippers, following toward the direction of the shadowy figure, not altogether sure of where that thing was leading him to, until he heard the click of a door being opened and shut. Only one door in that portion of the house ever remained closed, so that he knew, in an instant, where this burglar had taken him, and he knew his grandmother would not be happy about it.

CHAPTER SIX

SOME DANGEROUS SECRET

✦

T he door was unbolted.

He tried at the handle, turning it with care. Something moved within the room, it had heard him. Now he could no longer come at his intruder by surprise, and was therefore in more imminent danger, he thought.

Nevertheless, trying in a hurry to regain the upper hand, Timothy quickly pushed the door, flinging it open. He felt across the wall as if his life had depended on it, and switched on the light, but saw no one.

His voice wavered. "I'm not afraid of you," he managed to say, somewhat untruthfully, and gripping more tightly to the silvery candlestick holder in his hands.

There was no clear response, the room still appeared to be empty. But listening more carefully he thought to have heard a most unexpected sound, crying.

It was true, he was sure of it. Timothy heard the noise of gentle girlish sobs coming from across the room, possibly from behind his grandmother's large writing desk. Could it be that the hidden burglar had only been faking these sounds to throw him off his guard? That, however, seemed so absurdly unlikely that Timothy didn't give it much more thought, and instead went to go investigate this unsuspected sniffling. And what he found was a sad-looking blonde haired girl, dressed in a Mayfield school uniform. She was sobbing irreparably, clutching onto her knees with her head lowered, and seated in a ball underneath his grandmother's desk. (This was not the sort of bravery that Barbara had hoped for.)

"Who are you? And what are you doing in my house?" Timothy asked, rather reasonably to the girl beneath the desk.

"This is *your* house?" she asked in return, looking surprised and wiping the streaks of tears from below her eyes, trying to appear more presentable.

"Well... no," he answered truthfully. "Actually, it's my grandmother's, [and then with some authority in his voice] but I am staying here for the whole summer."

Barbara sounded amazed by his answer.

"And you're not afraid of her?" she asked him.

Timothy laughed heartily. "So says the girl who's been sneaking around our house in the middle of the night..." he grinned.

Barbara did not appreciate being laughed at, or about. And therefore, sitting up taller, more grown-up like, after managing to wipe nearly all the moisture from her eyes, she protested, "It's not like I'd wanted to."

To Timothy, the young girl seemed frustrated with him now, and he was smart enough to realize that he would probably not come to any good ends by picking fun at her, and as such, he decided to go about things by a different route.

"Alright, why not tell me why you *are* here then?" he said, having a seat behind the desk, legs crossed, to hear her side of the story as it were. "And why, on earth, I should be frightened of my own grandmother?"

This new approach seemed to work better for both of them, and Barbara did like being offered the opportunity to explain herself. However, first she'd needed to make sure they were "safe", as she called it, and refused to begin her story until Timothy had gone to switch off the main light, and had got for them two small candles instead. (This was so that Matilde Wolcott, who very well might go wandering through the halls in the middle of the night, would not by chance see drifts of light coming from within her forbidden attic study.)

These preparations took some time, but only because Timothy had to silently hunt around, in a pitch dark house, for a set of matches. Yet, eventually all was ready, and the two unlikely companions sat behind the desk, both holding lighted candles that washed a flickering glow onto their faces.

Here, and as follows, more or less, is what Barbara had said that night (with some of the more reliable information being added to help fill the gaps in her understanding of it):

For many years, it had been common knowledge amongst the girls at Mayfield that Delany Calbefur had been murdered. While the surviving governesses and the schoolmasters all seemed detached from reality, completely denying that any such murder had ever taken place, the girls at Mayfield knew better.

And while, for a long time, the true nature of that crime had remained a mystery, the students on the grounds of Mayfield would receive a yearly reminder, a quick flash of light through the high gable window, annually, just after midnight. (Or more precisely, exactly three hundred and sixty-five days from the time and date of Delany's first disappearance, an unearthly shot of light would shine out from that tiny window, which some girls had thought to be Delany's ghost come back to haunt what was once known as the old Greyford house: First named for businessman and collector, Arthur Greyford, but was now renamed for its new owner.)

[Here Timothy interrupted her telling to say that she was, "silly to fall for such a story like that." And that he didn't believe in ghosts. Yet to her own defense, Barbara was quick to say that she didn't believe in ghosts either, and that she was just repeating what she had heard.]

And so as the years passed, the legend of Delany Calbefur's murder, and the variations of it, became simply that, a legend. Growing ever more conjectured and imaginative, the truer nature of that crime being lost to history, until one day. Until the day that Mattie Hardy came back to Mayfield, as a grown woman, as Mrs. Matilde Wolcott, and had snatched up the old Greyford home for herself, along with its tangled history of murder. At which point, the flashes of light became more regular, and the truth about Timothy's grandmother had at last been revealed.

"Matilde Wolcott killed her best friend, and hid the evidence in the attic gable," she said at the end of her stories, drawing out the words rather creepily.

"You're lying," he retorted.

"Don't blame me. I'm just repeating what I heard," she replied.

Timothy's face made a frowned expression. "Well it's your fault for believing such rubbish," he muttered, looking cross. Which was clearly seen, even by pale candlelight, so that Barbara could tell her story was not well liked.

"And, by the way, what are you doing snooping in the attic here, if you're so scared of her?" Timothy continued.

Barbara did not like the tone in his voice, but chose to overlook it.

"I had to," she admitted. And she went on further to explain the rule for "first-yearers", and how she'd been pestered about it all year long, and how that this night had been the last night of the school year, her final chance to prove she was not frightened.

It seemed like a reasonable enough explanation, except that Timothy still did not take well to this girl barging in at all hours of the night, to accuse his family of murder.

"Sounds like a made-up story to me," he finally said, with half his wick already melted down to the bottom.

There was a silence, and then Barbara's eyes widened with a clever gleam, like she was going to enjoy what she was about to say.

"Yah," she blurted quickly. "Well if you're such a smarty, then tell me, where does the light come from?"

Timothy was puzzled, and his expression gave him away.

"Someone's got to be turning it on," she continued. "If your grandmother's not a murderer [and Barbara leaned forward over the flickering candle flame to make her point], then where's the entrance to the gable?"

(It should be noted that Barbara had asked a very decent question, so that, furthermore, she should be commended for her good sense of direction and logic. For truly said, that attic study was the highest and nearest room in the house, to the gable in question. So that, if there were going to be an entrance to it at all, it would have to be found there, but here in this forbidden attic study there was no entrance to be seen. And who keeps a hidden room, unless it had contained some dangerous secret? Or so were Barbara's thoughts on the matter.)

Howbeit, Timothy would not bear such wild accusations to be made about his close relations. And so, by ever dimming candlelight, the pair set about to prove their respective points, and thusly, by elimination, disproving the other's. But what they found was nothing at all like they had expected.

Hidden in a greenish-tinted old bottle, and rolled up like a shipwreck note was a handwritten letter, very ornately and beautifully scripted using an inkwell pen. Timothy unraveled the letter, holding it up to the candlelight as Barbara read in gasping whispers the contents of that note.

Dearest Mattie,

As you well know, tomorrow is Corwan's birthday celebration, and there will be music, and a parade, and a festival in his honor. And while I do respect your decision to stay on Earth for the summer, with your grandson, I would selfishly hope you might reconsider and come back just this once more for the party. It would mean so much to him, and to all of us, and to me.

And although it is not beneath my stature to beg, I shall try to restrain myself. The choice is yours. For always your friend.

And it was signed with elegant penmanship:

Her Majesty the Queen,

Delany

"You know what this means?" Barbara said, with wide-eyed amazement. "Delany Calbefur is still alive. Your grandmother's not a murder after all."

"It's more than that," Timothy spoke up, pointing to the contents of the letter. "She may still be alive, but she's not still *on Earth*."

CHAPTER SEVEN
THE HIDDEN ROOM
✦

F ootsteps.

Footsteps out in the hall, climbing a brief set of stairs to the forbidden attic study. Almost caught.

They puffed out their candles and Timothy had the forethought to re-roll the letter, sliding it back into the bottle.

"Hide," Barbara whispered, motioning for Timothy to follow her underneath the desk. It was not a very thought out plan, and an uncomfortably tight squeeze. In fact, Timothy was about to ask if she wouldn't mind moving her elbow, when suddenly the door opened, and Barbara shushed him to be quiet.

A desk lamp was lighted and its shadows played across the upstairs attic. The greenish hued bottle was lifted and the rolled letter slid out into Matilde's hands, then silence. From his poor hiding place, crouched beneath the desk, Timothy thought the silence might be because his grandmother had taken the time to reread her friend's mysterious note, which was the case.

The old woman reached her hand around the table, barely missing Timothy's shoulder, as she felt for the drawer handle. A slip of white writing paper, and a pen scribbled out her message. She wrapped it up quickly, pushing it back into the bottle with the palm of her hand.

His grandmother's footsteps came pacing behind the desk, and stood before a tall wooden bookshelf. From where the pair sat, the two trespassers huddled beneath the writing desk, they were in very real danger of being seen, but fortunately the feet never turned toward their direction.

Scraping across the attic floor, that massive bookcase began to move, and then suddenly his grandmother's feet lifted up softly, disappearing into nothing. (Except that they hadn't actually disappeared into nothing, but into the secret gable room.)

"Let's get out of here," Timothy whispered, as faintly as he could.

"What? And miss this?" Barbara replied, springing out from underneath the desk, and in the low lit attic study, the two curious intruders went on their toes toward an unexpected little window that had been, for some reason, hidden behind his grandmother's bookshelf.

(Dear reader, you must allow them their surprise at this moment. For though you may have read the first of these adventures, and will know quite well what to expect behind that tiny window curtain. Yet notwithstanding, here at this point, Barbara and Timothy knew very little about globe travel, nor had they any clue of what they might find. And the entire event: the flecks of starlight on their faces, the sight of Matilde Wolcott turning a small brass crank at the side of a peculiar ancient looking globe, the bands of light that spun outward, splashing against the high walls of that circular room, all of it was so new it burned inside of them, and the most bizarre, yet beautiful, otherworldly occurrence that either had yet known.)

When, after some more determined turning of that seemingly common looking brass crank, when finally Matilde looked satisfied with her efforts, and when the globe glowed brightly, she reached her fingers gently into the green bottle, pulling outward a little pointed tip of paper. She touched the slightest edge of that paper, which she held still within the bottle, and that bottle within her hands, the smallest sliver of writing paper hit the globe and a flash of golden-white light surged upward from the globe, as if the wind had carried it.

From their point of view, even within the other room, gazing inward, they could now hear a high piercing ringing sound. The bottle began to float, out of Matilde's hand, up into the air, with what seemed to be a circle of pure visible sun rays inclosing around it.

Then a blinding cannon of explosive light, and the bottle was gone. It was possibly flown into what seemed to be a massive lifelike painting that looked to stretch the length of one whole wall, but the intensity of the light made it hard to know for sure.

However, that was not the worst of it, at present they couldn't see anything at all. The flash of brightness, into their low lit room shocked and temporarily blurred their vision, like the brilliance of a thousand candles all at once.

Timothy rubbed his eyes, squinting, but to no effect. Footsteps, again.

"Timothy Rodger Hayfield!" he heard his grandmother calling out his full given birth name. "I'd very well hope you can explain to me what you're doing here in my study, and who this young girl is, here in my house after midnight... and you'd better do it quick."

He rubbed his eyes again, just able to make out the shape of his grandmother's very irritated face, glaring at him from inside the window room.

"Is it too late for us to go to the party?" he asked, not knowing what else he could possibly say for himself at that moment.

"Ha!" Barbara blurted out a laugh, but almost as quickly as she had done so she threw her hand up to cover her mouth.

And it was much to both of their benefits that Timothy's grandmother, Matilde Wolcott, was no stranger to getting in trouble herself. And moreover, if he could have seen it at the time, he would have noticed a slight girlish grin flicker across his grandmother's not so wrinkled face.

CHAPTER EIGHT
A WARNING

✦

A bout an hour before the first clips of sunrise were scheduled to spread out across the trees and countryside of Mayfield, a very weary, unslept Barbara Cholley was finally sent away to sneak back to her dormitory, just in time for her last day of school for the term, and a test in Algebra that she'd been vastly unprepared for.

In truth, she might have left much sooner, for it took that poor girl barely a few minutes to introduce herself, and to describe in full how she had come to be there that night, and also for Timothy to explain his involvement in the matter.

But what had taken far longer were Matilde's stories: of the window room and Delany Calbefur, and of Gleomu, and princes, and kingdoms, and worlds beyond our own. They were all treasured stories which Matilde had long wished to tell, but that she had been forced to keep secret from nearly every person for whom she had cared most deeply. And until that night, she had been the last remaining person on earth who had known of that hidden room, and it felt freeing for her to tell of it.

Though nearing the end of her stories, by then, Timothy was practically shamefully begging to be taken along to King Corwan's birthday celebration, and Barbara must have said three or four times over, without even realizing that she'd been repeating herself, that how much fun a king's birthday must be.

So that just after all of Matilde's stories were told for the night, by that time Barbara had finally mustered the courage to ask for herself, a request that had caught both of her new hosts completely off their guard.

"I'd also like to come along, as well, Mrs. Wolcott," she said, tucking her hair shyly behind her ear, "...if it's not too much trouble."

Both Timothy and Matilde were quite shocked by this request. "But what about your parents, dear?" Matilde asked her in return. (Considering rightly, that that morning began the last day of courses for the term.)

"Oh, they won't mind," Barbara answered back, like she could be certain of it, but seeing that this response had needed further explanation, she went on to describe her most inevitable plans for the summer.

For you see, Barbara Cholley was what some of the other girls at Mayfield had distastefully liked to refer to as an "orphan". But not a real orphan, mind you. By the way that they used the word, it meant someone whose parents did not care enough for them to bring them home over holidays.

Though truthfully, Barbara's parents were not all that bad, as people go, (they gave to favorite charities, and were well liked at society functions) but they were horrid parents, and more specifically Barbara's mother, although neither was really all that affectionate. And consequently, they had both much rather preferred to spend this particular summer in Madrid, than to be bothered by their only daughter.

Howbeit, in response to her request, Matilde had said she'd needed more time to think it over; And furthermore, that it was ultimately not her choice to make, that all new travelers to Gleomu would first need "royal approval", but that she would inform them of the King's decision before nightfall.

The early morning hours on the hills of Mayfield were beginning to wane. Soon the sun would be visible across the field, giving Barbara a ghastly hard time if she'd wanted to make it safely back to her dormitory without being noticed.

Even still, Matilde knew it was not fair or right for her to simply leave her new novice globe travelers there that evening without a proper caution for the true dangers it presented, and so before she had finished completely she gave them this solemn warning (possibly brought about by Timothy, who had joined in with Barbara to say how much "fun" this adventure was going to be, and how all his friends back home would surely be jealous if they'd heard about it):

"This is not a toy, my dear, or something to be done lightly. This is a very dangerous secret we all now hold... and it must remain a secret if we are to have any safety in it." And then the old woman, who had once been Mattie Hardy, reached across the kitchen table dramatically, taking ahold of their hands tightly. "To travel beyond our world is to change this present one forever, and I shall give you both till the end of the day to reconsider."

Then they all sat up from the table, and Barbara was shuffled out the door and away from Wolcott Manor, the damp morning dew just beginning to feel palpable against her skin.

Perhaps that old house was even more foreboding and mysterious than she had first realized. And that morning, she slept through the last fifteen minutes of her algebra exam, dreaming of kings' birthday cakes and women in ankle length festival dresses, where everything was most regal and proper. Till that moment, it was the grandest dream she'd ever remembered, and well worth the scolding she'd received from Schoolmaster Collins.

CHAPTER NINE

A BETTER DRESS

✦

H orse hoofs glistened off the wet grasses, striking the plains, nearing the distant city of Ismere with a determined fury. Both horse and rider looked as though they had long ago ceased resting. The animal's brown and ashy muscular hide blended evenly into the rider's own tanned skin, and together they galloped in stride toward the northern gate of the great sand-stoned city as one, resolute in their natures.

The city walls were almost barely unseen, like a small pebble on the horizon, beneath the gaze of much larger distant mountains. The thin light of early dawn reflected behind the snowcaps, and moved delicately upwards in the morning sky, until it mirrored against a cool and peaceful lake near the city. Ismere, the jewel of Gleomu and its principal city, stood as an ever vigilant watchman over those long undivided plains.

And the horse and his rider continued on, hoping to make their rest in the King's palace by midmorning.

It was most beneficial for all involved that Mrs. Wolcott was on good terms with the proprietors and schoolmasters at Mayfield, especially with Head Governess Leeching, who thought it to be a perfectly splendid idea to house one of her "orphans" at the Wolcott house for the summer. "One less brat to worry about," were the Governess's exact words.

And so it happened, that by late afternoon Barbara had packed up most of her things into a large clasped suitcase, and after wishing her goodbyes to the few somber "orphan" girls who'd remained, she carried her weighty luggage, heaving and dragging it the last bit of the way up the dirt footpath toward the old manor on the hill. And she was warmly welcomed in, by that same old woman whom she'd just hours earlier mistakenly believed to be an evil murderess.

"Are you sure of this, my dear?" Matilde asked her wide-eyed and hopeful looking new house guest.

"Yes, of course, Mrs. Wolcott," answered Barbara. "It feels like you've rescued me from the most boring holiday of my life," she continued, setting her overpacked luggage down in the entryway of her new summer home.

Opening the door down the hall, Timothy burst from his room. He was busy fastening the last collar button on a forest green tunic, and looking rather respectable, although that was soon ended.

"Is *that* what you're going to wear to the party?" Timothy prodded in an unwittingly rude manner, to Barbara who stood at their doorstep, still dressed in her school uniform, which was measurably shabby by comparison.

"Nooo..." she answered back, slightly rolling her eyes. And his grandmother gave him a less than approving look as well, although Timothy had no idea what for.

"Come on," Matilde said reaching for Barbara's hand. "I have whole wardrobes filled with gowns, from my early years in Gleomu. Surely we can find something that'll fit."

And with that, the two girls went rushing upstairs to see what they might find. Leaving Timothy, alone at the base of the stairs, thinking over how he shall never be able to understand women. (Though granted he did not stand around idly, being bothered by it for very long, not as adventurous as this evening was supposed to be.)

Much later that night, the three travelers stood in the window room, as the vivid starlight and glowing vignettes of Gleomu poured out of that giant lifelike painting onto their washed and ready faces.

After many failed attempts, and after hours of searching through old closet drawers, and through chests tucked away in seldom visited corners of that great house, the two women had found astoundingly lovely dresses to wear, ones most suited for royal company; Matilde wore a watery lake blue gown, and her hair was elegantly braided, and Barbara, quite determined to make her best impression, had scoured every closet and wardrobe, till she had come upon a dress that was just her size, a crimson and snow white renaissance-styled dress with golden stitching, of real gold, and a reddened sash in her hair of the same color as her dress.

And when all was prepared, they were arrived at last, in the dark of that hidden gable room, as Matilde gave her final instructions about globe travel. Telling her eager companions that they were free to explore the palace and the city of Ismere, and free to roam around that world to their heart's content. Except that, when their time was up they would need to be near her, or else they'd run the very real risk of being left behind.

"Forever?" Barbara asked, thinking she might need to reconsider agreeing to such a dangerous, or potentially permanent, summer's holiday.

"No," the old woman chuckled at her. "I'll come back for you... But still, it's no fun to be left alone, just take my word for it."

"How long have we got for exploring, again?" Timothy questioned, also seeming nervous at the thought of being stranded on a distant planet.

"Three days, exactly," his grandmother answered, pointing once more toward the dials on the globe that set their time. "Do I need to repeat the process for you?" she asked him.

"I suppose... but maybe more slowly this time?" he replied.

Matilde was very fond of her grandson, and did not mind, in the least, repeating herself. "Alright... once more," she said, and went back through each step again, demonstrating and announcing each movement as she did so, and ending lastly with the turning of the brass crank to charge the globe. (And she let each one have their own try at the crank to get the feel of it. As Timothy began turning the unassuming old brass crank that mechanism started awakening, it twirled and ticked and glowed from deep inside its center.)

And their guide leaned over the globe, pointing toward a specific location on its face.

"See where my finger is?" she asked them, when at last she had concluded her lesson. And they both nodded to show that they had. "You must touch, right... here," she motioned, being infinitely precise in her movements.

The tenderest tip of her finger hit the body of the globe, and a wave of light struck their faces. They were being lifted into the air, holding with fingers clasped onto Matilde's slightly wrinkled hands.

"Why three days?" Barbara yelled out as an orb of light condensed around them. "I thought we were just going to a party."

Matilde smiled as if she had known better than they.

"This is a king's birthday, my dear."

Flash!

The gable room had disappeared, and what remained was speed, and infinite light. (And although Timothy would swear against it, both he and Barbara had screamed more loudly than they would have liked.)

CHAPTER TEN
SOMETHING SO BEAUTIFUL

The three catapulted through the universe at a velocity that, only a few minutes prior, neither young traveler had thought humanly possible. Inside their orb was neither wind nor noise, and the stars moved by in burning silence. To their left, they soared past a mammoth gaseous planet, orbited by several reddish colored moons.

"Is that... that," asked Timothy, trying to recall the exact right planet's name in his excitement. "...Jupiter, grandmum?"

"No, deary," she answered, still holding tightly to both of their hands. "We're many solar systems away from that by now, and nearly beyond our portion of the galaxy."

And Matilde, who had always been aptly good at science, even since she'd been in primary school, could not, by habit, continue on without stating this fact, one that had been obvious only to her, "...and besides, at this time of the year, Jupiter would have been in the opposite direction."

And for a long while they traveled through the expanse of space without saying much of anything,

41

until Barbara could no longer contain the awe she felt.

"No way..." she said, softly disbelieving.

Her mouth hung open in wonderment, as their orb rocketed through a four sun solar system (which, if you've the chance to see one up close, is actually quite marvelous, and is mechanically much more complex than our own single sun system: which in itself should only be classified as "simple" by comparison.)

Barbara reached to tap Timothy on the shoulder. "Do you believe this?" she asked him.

But he'd looked as overawed by it as she had. "I'm trying to," he answered.

Yet after some more minutes of flying, his face grew tight with what seemed like concern, as if he were forming a necessary question, or like he'd been slowly growing mad about something, only something he could not exactly put a finger on, nor give a name to.

"Why not tell mother and father about this?" he blurted quickly, like his words were uncontrollable. " ...Or anyone else for that matter. Did grandfather know about this?" he questioned. And muttered finally, "Seems awfully selfish to keep such a great thing hidden away from people."

Barbara could not believe how Timothy could behave so rudely, and her eyes showed it clearly. Although, he might have been partially justified, at this moment, in a way that Barbara would not have realized. For you see, he had all of a sudden just got the unshakeable feeling that he, along with every member of his immediate family, had been lied to their whole lives, and it was a most unlikeable feeling.

Matilde knew one day she would have to explain her actions, and had been preparing herself for it as much as possible. However, she did not expect to be so saddened by it, when the time came.

And holding more tightly onto her grandson's hand, she answered, "Your grandfather knew about the window room. It was one of his favorite places..." Her eyes began to well with tears, a little.

"He adored our trips to Gleomu, and the special quarters set aside for us in the palace. And he loved staying late in the banquet hall, with a pipe in one hand, sharing stories, and swapping medical knowledge with the local physicians, even though I think he'd aways learned more from them, than they did from him," she sighed, seeming to be deeply affected by her memories. Her lips closed firmly, like she did not wish to speak anymore of it. For, although these were fond images and stories to recall, they'd now held a special burden for her, whenever she'd brought them to mind, a type of sadness she thought she must now learn to endure.

And so she continued on about a different matter, saying, "For a long time I'd thought to tell your mother and uncles, once they were older. But then the war happened, and we knew, Wilbur and I, that such a knowledge would be even far more dangerous than we'd first realized."

Barbara looked broken, herself, for Matilde's pain, but could not comprehend on her own, how such a beautiful thing could be at all as dangerous as she said it was.

"Mrs. Wolcott," she said to gather the old woman's attention. "How could such a good thing, like this, be so dangerous?" She asked this as their golden orb began to slow, descending through the morning clouds of that new world.

And Matilde looked at Barbara, and knew her answer without thinking, because for her it had been hard learned.

"Dear child, in my own lifetime, I have seen cars strapped with artillery, and planes flown away on bombing missions..." she paused slightly, then continued being very sure and serious in her words, "And our hidden light travel is the grandest form of transportation our world has ever known, and therefore our most uncontrollable weapon."

Their feet touched down gently on the well-trimmed grass of the palace gardens, and there were all the things that Timothy and Barbara had hoped to see: hanging gardens, marble fountains, and hedges cut to form the shapes of mythical creatures, palace officials, and guards dressed in full readied armor.

Near one of the fountains, at the center of a large crowd, sat an elegant king and queen, wearing thin crowns of gold set with precious stones, and both in splendid courtly attire.

If Timothy were to be the last of his family to know about the window room, then he would do his duty well, he thought. He would be its protector.

CHAPTER ELEVEN
THE KING'S BIRTHDAY

W hen the King saw that his guests had arrived he burst from his seat. He had been entertained for the greater part of that morning by a performance in His Majesty's honor, a very elaborate depiction of some of he and his late father's grandest military victories. Except all this entertainment seemed not to matter, as soon as he saw the three light travelers descending from the crisp cool autumn sky, on the morning of his birthday.

He flung his arms wide, like he could hug a giant. By the King's stature you would not have taken him for an old man, if not for the long strands of grey in his beard. His back stood straight, and arms and chest burly, as regal and firm as you would hope a king to be. Deeply his voice bellowed out across the lawn, halting the minstrels' music as he yelled, "Mattie! It's so good of you to join us," as he came rushing up from his seat.

Timothy's grandmother bowed a stately curtsy.

"Your Majesty," Matilde said as she lowered (leading Barbara to follow after her example, and Timothy to try at an awkward but suitable bow).

"A most happy birthday," Matilde continued, rising as the King came up quickly to greet her, with the Queen rushing close after him, holding the hem of her dress up above her feet as she ran.

"Mattie!" the Queen cheered, throwing her arms around the neck of her lifelong friend.

"And this must be your grandson?" she said, with a joyful expectation in her voice.

"Yes," Matilde answered coming to stand behind her grandson, placing both her hands on his shoulders. "This is Timothy," she said, as the Queen stooped down to have a better look at him.

"Even more handsome than I'd imagined him to be," the Queen said, touching her white gloved hand to his cheek (which made Timothy subtly blush, even as much as he'd tried to avoid it).

"And this is his friend, Barbara, whom I'd told you about," Matilde spoke up again, motioning toward the young girl beside her, who was dressed in a fitting velvety red and white gown (and who at that moment was thinking how grateful she was to have found a better dress than her school uniform for the occasion).

"My, aren't you lovely," issued the Queen, running the cup of her hand delicately down the length of Barbara's long blonde hair.

To Barbara, she had thought then that she had never before seen a woman so fair and proper as this queen was. And Timothy thought, that knowing from the stories he'd heard, how that King Corwan and Queen Delany were roughly his grandmother's age, how odd it was that neither of them looked as particularly aged as

46

you'd expect them to be. And he'd concluded that there must be something in the world of Gleomu that had caused this[x].

But what had begun so well that morning, suddenly took a turn for the worse. And Timothy, who had for a long time prided himself on his skills of observation, knew there must have been something terribly amiss in the kingdom to warrant his grandmother's reaction.

Not long after they'd arrived, the King and Queen were called away from the party to attend to some urgent matter, and not but a few seconds later Timothy's grandmother, along with a few hand-selected military officers, were also taken to a secretive quarters within the palace, and there they stayed for nearly an hour.

Both Timothy and Barbara had tried to follow after them, but were unallowed, and so they passed the time mulling around the palace gardens. During their wait, they took to examining the intricate marble statues and found, instead, something even more spectacular, a hedge dragon that was cut so precisely that the leaves

---

[x] While some scholars have argued back and forth, about what this factor might be that causes such long life in Gleomu: pointing toward the presence of some mineral in the water, or the absence of certain enzymes, it has been my own personal opinion that such a difference between our worlds is met on a much larger scale, that it is not such a miniscule difference as it is a massive one; That the entire atmosphere of Gleomu is vastly different from our own, and much more suitable for human life. Or else, that it is a much younger world, as planets go, and still in its prime.

took the shapes of scales covering its back and wings, and when the breeze would blow in you would swear it moved.

All things considered, they rather enjoyed their time exploring the gardens, and then watching the royal performers as they aptly succeeded in trying to keep the King's elaborately dressed guests entertained, and just before Matilde returned, Barbara happened to overhear a pair of guards speaking in hushed voices near the entry doors to the palace, saying that, "a messenger had just arrived." Although that was all that Barbara could strain to hear, because they were speaking rather quietly; And since she did not, after all, want to appear overly nosey on her first day in a king's palace, she left them alone, and ran off to tell Timothy what she'd heard.

But almost as soon as Barbara could share the news, Matilde reemerged, looking distressed. She said, something had come up that required her attention, but assured them that this needn't spoil their first day in Gleomu, nor the King's birthday celebration, and she sent them away under the good care of Asa, the Queen's third eldest son, to attend the street festival, and to sit with the royal family during the parade. (Which, as you should know, is something that is most looked forward to every year, drawing in a worthy crowd from every far corner of the kingdom.)

Though at first, Timothy, and later Barbara, had refused to go, once they saw how his grandmother had intended to spend her day, locked up in the palace, to discuss some matters with the King's generals, all of whom she'd known by name and station, and seemed to be quite familiar with.

"We won't go," Barbara said finally, not wishing to stay exactly, yet not willing to leave Mrs. Wolcott alone, by herself for the day.

And Timothy, seizing on an opportunity to get down to the truth of all this, butted in, "Yes, not until you tell us what's going on."

Yet, as anyone may have guessed, that only aggravated Matilde all the more, who assured them that they would do her no good just loitering about; And that it was not "her place" to tell, and that the King would make his announcement soon enough, and that they needn't worry for her sake.

And so, with nothing left to protest, the two were whisked away, to enjoy a day of fun and festivities: along with fire eaters, and spiced teas with wafer candies, and all that made the King's birthday celebration something to be looked forward to each year. And as much as either would have hated to have admitted it, they did not concern themselves very much with Mrs. Wolcott, until they returned again to the palace that evening, when they saw Timothy's grandmother seated in a place of honor, at the head of the banquet hall, alongside the Queen, Delany, and wearing (as Barbara had pointed out), a thin gold band around her forehead, as well, set with jewels in a style similar, yet not exact, to the Queen's own crown.

"Why on earth would she be wearing that?" Timothy thought.

Yet he refrained his urge to ask the question aloud, in case there were some obvious answer he'd overlooked;

And also, so he would not be seen as foolish in front of the King's son, Asa, who'd sat beside them in the banquet hall, still graciously acting as their guide, on this their first day in a new and unfamiliar world.

CHAPTER TWELVE
A MESSAGE
✦

W hile the main course was being served (which if you would like to know was roast duck, and something like a plum pudding), King Corwan rose up to make an announcement.

First, he thanked all those at the banquet for coming to his birthday celebration, and he thanked them for their generous gifts and for the day's festivities, which would "long be remembered," but he told them that sadly further enjoyments would need to be cut short, for there was distressing news from the northern country that had needed his immediate and full attention.

And these were the King's words, seasoned with the gravity of the situation: He informed them that a messenger had just rode in from the northern front, carrying news that the fort city of Hrim had been fired upon nearly a week prior. An audible gasp could be heard as the King spoke, and as he paused it grew into an uproar, a few calling for war, or blaming the attack on kingdoms or peoples that Timothy had never heard of, but finally, Corwan, raising his hands, called them all to order and continued.

Saying that, on the night of the attack, late after midnight, a lone archer fired over the gates a single flaming arrow. The damage was not severe, but once the flames were extinguished the night watchmen found a letter, rolled into the arrow's hollowed metal shaft. And holding that same letter in his hands, the King read it aloud for all in attendance:

To Corwan, son of Reuel, King of Gleomu -

The King of Earth is alive, yet he will not remain as such, unless his Queen is brought alone to the fort of Hrim, and by the 15th day of Kislev, to await my further instruction.

If you try to secure her, or if she escapes back to Earth, I will slay both Earth's King and Gleomu's, and burn the city of Ismere to the ground.

Let this stand as a warning.

This letter bore no signature, and caused a violent upheaval in what had been a peaceful celebration. The King's guests exploded in unrelenting yells and outbursts. Some, mostly noblemen, cautioned that they should do all as the ransom letter requested. While others, more so members of council and generals, confessed that they would rather die first.

In the confusion and havoc of that moment, Barbara spoke loudly into Timothy's ear, to get above the noise, asking, "What would someone *here* want with the Queen?" her face bewildered. Yet, Timothy was able to decipher the letter's true meaning, and therefore answered her question correctly.

"Not the Queen of England," he said, looking also stunned himself. "I doubt they've even ever heard of her. They want the Queen *of Earth*."

But Barbara still did not follow his meaning, and so he said it more plainly. "The Queen of Earth, my grandmother."

"Oh..." Barbara said loudly, still trying to be heard above the noise of that chaotic banquet hall, and now at last understanding the full intent of the letter.

And a few seconds later a thought came into her head, and she asked a fairly sensible question, but one that was most obviously ill timed considering the circumstances, and judging by Timothy's frowning response.

"Does that make you a prince, then?" she asked.

CHAPTER THIRTEEN
THE TRUTH

Wilbur Wolcott was dead, Timothy's grandfather, or maybe it should be better said that at least on Earth, rather, he was believed to be.

Nearly a full year had passed by then, but Timothy could still remember the pungent odor of funeral flowers in his nostrils, the way that all the observers at the memorial service had draped themselves in black, and had all worn a dreadfully similar somber expression.

In his mind, he could recall a fragment of each speech given that day. He remembered the image of his grandmother crying. All these thoughts led to only one obvious conclusion: That, on Earth, Wilbur Wolcott was dead.

And yet, Timothy had come very far from Earth by now, and in Gleomu, his grandfather, King Wilbur of Earth, was not dead, but kidnapped. Which is a state very much different from death, but still not something that could have been easily explained, or even believed. And so Timothy understood her reasoning, why his grandmother had kept such a secret hidden from the family. Howbeit, at present, he was no longer on Earth, and would no longer be babied, as he saw it, and on his first day away from our world he thought he'd very much deserved a true answer for what had really happened.

Which is why he snuck from his quarters that same night, toward where he remembered his grandmother's room to be. But almost before he could round the first corner, he heard a door gently shut behind him, and he caught the noise of girlish footsteps that came running up to meet him.

It was Barbara, wrapped up in a full length nightdress, her feet pattering in comfortable palace slippers.

"What do you want?" Timothy asked, voicing his words more rudely than he would normally. (And this was because he'd also thought he'd deserved not to be bothered.)

She ran up, and matched his quickening pace.

"I want to know what's going on, same as you," she answered back.

And knowing that nothing he might say would dissuade her, they both went searching together through the palace corridors, till they found a familiar passageway, and the thick auburn colored door of his grandmother's room. He gave a forceful knock.

A fire was lit, and the glow of it waved in and out along the walls, and across the cherry dyed satin sheets of a four posted bed. And there by the fire, Matilde, the Queen of Earth, had been wrapped up in a woolen blanket, and looked as though she'd been anticipating them, her new late night guests.

And without much ado, nor without even being properly asked, she began to speak her peace that night, the truth of what had happened nearly a year before to Timothy's grandfather, while both her listeners sat almost unbreathing.

Here are the words that Matilde, the Queen of Earth, spoke that night. And she began, first pouring each of her guests a cup of tea:

"Your grandfather simply loved the harvest festivals near Bearu... and the kingdom was at peace. We had no cause for concern, when traveling alone to the annual festivals, without royal guards." [Here Matilde took a gentle sip of her mint leaf tea to settle herself, and Timothy thought she'd looked upset, and possibly to the point of tears, if she were pressed to continue.]

"It's alright... You can stop, if you'd like," Timothy said, leaning forward to comfort his grandmother.

"No, no. You should hear the truth," and she took a shallow gulp of air, forcing herself onward.

Then she told them how King Corwan had pressing matters in the High Council to attend to at that time, and therefore Queen Delany, Wilbur, and herself had left alone on horseback, riding the week's long journey, over the Theydor river, to the festivals; And how they'd slept in the fields, and rode on in the cooler parts of the day.

However, this perplexed Barbara, who had not yet understood the comfort of sleeping in anything but a nice warm bed.

"Why not just use the globe, and fly there?" she asked.

Matilde smiled. "Dear, you can miss so much of life by hurrying."

And she went on to tell how the events that year were spectacular, even better than expected, but on their return trip they had camped for the night in an open glade, just half a day's ride from Ismere.

"...We could have made it there, if we'd just rode faster." Matilde paused to hold back her frustration, obviously still mad at herself for the things she had no power over.

Their storyteller fiddled with the folds of her blanket as they sat near the fire, soaking in its heat. "In the morning we were ambushed," she continued very plainly. "Some judged our attackers for common horse thieves, but I've never been so sure of that."

"How could you tell they weren't?" Barbara interrupted.

"Well... because of how they fought, more like trained mercenaries than horse thieves," she replied.

At that, both of her young listeners were completely befuddled.

"You fought with them?" Timothy blurted out unbelievingly (as I suspect most would).

"What?" This seemed to rattle his grandmother's usually mild manners. "I'm old, but I'm not dead," she issued. "And when you've grown up as Del and I had, you'll learn to fend for yourself rather quickly," she insisted.

And being pressed, she went on further to tell how the thieves had lurched upon them, trying to kidnap all of them, but said that their attackers had most likely been foreigners, or else they would have known the Queen to be an expert swordsman, and herself to be a most skilled archer and quick with a dagger. And that, if they had been natives, they would have likely taken more care with their lives.

"But they stole Wilbur?" Barbara asked, seeming like she might, as well, begin to tear at the thought.

"Yes," Matilde answered, breathing a heavy sigh as if still angry, and maybe at herself.

Then, directing her attention toward Timothy, she continued, "Your grandfather was a decent scrapper, I'll grant him that, but he's always been more of a doctor than a warrior." She took another breath and a sip of soothing tea.

"And after all, being over the age of thirty by the time he'd first come to Gleomu, and during peacetime, he hadn't needed to develop his skills as intently, while Del and I had been raised with it."

Then she told how the few mercenaries that had survived the attack rode off on the royal horses, headed northward, but with no ransom for a year, she said that most in the kingdom had assumed the worst.

"Did *you?*" Barbara asked, sounding particularly caring.

Matilde sat back, widening her eyes, as though to keep her tears at bay.

"No, I've always tried to keep up hope... but I can't imagine what he's had to go through."

And she turned her head swiftly, looking into the low burning hearth, meaning to hide her tears, but what it had actually done was to let them sparkle, as the little droplets rolled down the thin lines of her face.

Timothy was no good at crying, nor at watching women cry, and so he meant to try to make it better. And he remembered his own mother, when they'd first thought his grandfather to have died, how she'd cried almost instantly and intermittently for several months, becoming less frequent as time moved along, and he was no good at that either.

"Don't worry, grandmother. We'll find him."

But this was less accepted than he had thought.

The old woman, Matilde Wolcott, Queen of Earth, jolted back toward their direction.

"No. Absolutely not," she said poignantly. "You're going home."

"But-"

Timothy tried to make his case, but Matilde wouldn't hear a word of it.

"No," she held up her finger to shush him. "How would your mother feel, if she knew I put you into such danger?" And she shook her grey streaked hair. "No, I will not lose a husband and a grandchild all within the same year."

Timothy pursed his lower lip upward when he heard this. He knew it was pointless to argue now, although he had wanted to. There was no avoiding it. It seemed he and Barbara's adventures and bravery in this new world were being cut short. And who would dare argue with the Queen of Earth?

CHAPTER FOURTEEN

THE COUNCIL

A t the center of the city, in the council building, by the following late morning, there were heated arguments in favor and against bending to any ransomer's requests, and more substantially against placing Queen Matilde willingly into any amount of peril.

However, and surprisingly to some, it was the Queen of Earth, herself, who'd stood up in opposition most vehemently and would not heed to any of their cautions, as she made her address before the council.

Timothy and Barbara sat in a section of the audience's seating reserved for high ranking dignitaries, and had both been fairly engrossed in the proceedings since just after breakfast. The expansive structure, with its grand bench seating, for the members of council, brimmed beyond capacity. The place was a bustle of activity and filled with ready spectators since the King had called for an emergency council meeting on the night before. And the noises of arguments and rebuttals seemed to swell more loudly as the day wore on.

One of the council members, bearded and portly in appearance, spoke out, offering his own advice. "Your Majesty," he said addressing Timothy's grandmother.

"With all due respect to your office, these kidnappers are very obviously laying a trap for us, and should we walk toward it blindly?" He took a large breath, most of it through his nose. "Wouldn't it be a more discriminating choice, to send out a battalion first, to search out their intentions, before allowing Your Excellency to be placed into harm's way?"

However, Matilde would hear none of this, and spoke nearly overtop of the man to get out her answer. Which she issued out, standing at the center of the court building and turning as she spoke, to be sure she was heard by all in attendance.

"Councilman, with all due respect, I will place myself into any harm that is required of me, as long as my husband's life is at stake." And then turning again, redirecting her attentions toward that specific council member, she said, "And if I shall not have the support of the King's army, then I will go at it alone."

Her voice was unwavering, and her warnings left any reluctant members of the council without nearly a choice but to side with the King's request for military intervention. Which was soon made much easier, when King Corwan suggested that this regiment be made up entirely of volunteers, which was met with unanimous support.

And just as the last councilman stood to give his vote, sealing their decision, Barbara leaned in, to whisper to Timothy, "Even for a fake queen, she's quite good at it."

Their last day in that world was much less dramatic, but a good amount more like what they had hoped their days to be like during their visit: A late breakfast of smoked salmon, hand squeezed juices, and fetra, a specialty dish of wild potatoes and herbs. (Which upon writing this sounds much less appealing than it tastes. And so, if you'll please, you may just have to take my word on it when I say that both young travelers helped themselves to second platefuls.)

And after breakfast, at the behest of adventure, they were sent on various trips throughout the city: a carriage ride through the merchant district, a walk atop the wide city walls to see the armaments, and then lunch in the main square, dancing, and a spectacular performance of juggling. And after what was a very full dinner, Barbara was whisked away by the Queen's three daughters (who in order of their ages are: Alethea, Amity, and lastly Pemberley, the youngest of her twelve brothers and sisters). That said, Barbara was stolen away for an evening of beauty treatments, that, I presume, nearly all women find invigorating. While Asa, the King's son, as a means of saving Timothy from such tortures, brought him to the main palace hall by torchlight to begin his training in the art of swordsmanship, a skill quite necessary for all respectable princes.

And yet, as one may not have anticipated, given

Timothy's more moderate stature, he, who'd spent a good portion of his childhood watching staged combat, as a tag-along on the set of many of his father's productions, he showed an instant knack for swordplay; Albeit still, understandably, many many years behind Asa's skill level and strength. And clearly seeing that with any flick of the wrist his mentor could easily unhand him (without Timothy even barely noticing what had happened), he was not too quick to forget his place as a pupil.

At the end of the night, the two left the great hall and went to go their separate ways. And Timothy, his arms fully wearied from hours of sparring, eagerly let his tired arms settle limply at his sides, once he was sure Asa had turned to go in the opposite direction, and could no longer see him. Although, in doing so, the flat of his palm grazed the handle of a sword. This startled him. He'd become completely unaware of it at his side, and he ran back to catch pace with his mentor.

"You forgot your extra sword," Timothy said, trying to sound much less winded than he may have actually been.

"Oh, *did I?*" Asa replied.

And Asa, pausing to stroke the front of his night black beard, but with an expression on his face as if he'd had some idea in his head all along, and had only been feigning at thoughts, knowing full well what he'd intended to do.

"You keep it," the King's son answered back. And in his deep voiced way of it, he said, "Consider it a gift, from one prince to another."

A emerald green hilt, with a woven band of gold around it. A flashy metal blade with the engraving of eagle wings etched onto its surface. Timothy had never owned a weapon before. And although he had always secretly wanted a sword of his own, he was never so foolish as to think his mother would have allowed him it, back home in London. And this new sword and sheath were a marker to Timothy that he was beginning to grow accustomed to his newly discovered princedom.

"If only I could be a prince in every world," he thought, as he drifted off to sleep.

And although Timothy, himself, would have found this childish to admit to: On his last night there in the palace, he slept with his new sword on his bed, resting its handle on a pillow for safe keeping. And all that night he dreamt of slaying beasts, and that the cut hedge dragon in the palace garden had come to life, and of glorious battles, and always with the truest of bravery, and finest valor, all things well befitting a prince of Earth.

CHAPTER FIFTEEN
THE REGIMENT
✦

A lmost as quickly as they set their steps on this new world it was time to say goodbye, and there were many fond farewells. Both young travelers had no less than begged to be left behind at the palace, but Matilde, the Queen, expressly forbade it. Saying, that if she were not able to be present to secure their safety entirely, then they would, both of them, need to be left in the safest place available to them, which plainly put was back home in Mayfield, where they had hoped to have escaped from for the summer, but those fair dreams had now seemed impossible.

And so, around midmorning, as the King's regiment was already prepared for their journey, and were receiving their commissioning at the northern gate, the King stood to give his address. And King Corwan thanked the men for their willingness, and made statements about their sacrifice and dedication, to volunteer as they had; There were thirty-nine men in total, saddled on horses, swords strapped onto their backs in preparation for the long ride ahead of them. Some of these volunteer soldiers being from the King's own palace guard, some generals (both old and young), some more brave council members, and the rest of the group were filled up with layman, (which is not something very unusual for Gleomu, and if I can be allowed a little bit of boredom I'd like to tell you why: You see, because the realm of Gleomu has enjoyed a history of relative peace, sometimes spanning nearly a century at a time without much war, if any at all, the ruling council had long, long ago developed a system for enlistment known as the citizen's army. Which, according to law, dictates that every able-bodied man, twice a year, must take a week's leave from his other duties, in order to train for battle, and in so doing, they have eliminated the need for a standing army, as most countries in our own world will have. Notwithstanding, the only ranks held on a full time basis are that of the generals, who facilitate training in times of peace, and direct conscription and troop's movements in times of war. Which then leaves the last and highest rank, in an active army, to the King, the General of Generals, as he is known by in wartime. It is a system for battle that has worked, without flaw, for generations, and by my judgement, is something I should like to see replicated here on Earth, although I am not so blind as to hope for it.

And, if I may add one more thing, the only time in history, to my knowledge, that this mandate of the citizen's army had been nullified was during the false reign of Faron, the King's wicked older brother. And I should suspect the reason for this being that only tyrants, as he was indeed, will fear the military strength of their subjects, and will work unrelentingly to deny them these abilities, in order to bolster their own stolen and misdirected powers. Such vicious men, we have seen and continue to see run rampant in our world, but my hope is that the likes of these shall never be welcomed in Gleomu.)

And now, again to our story: The only other volunteers there that morning not yet mentioned, on the hillside by the northern gate, were two of the King's sons: Asa, who had served as a royal host for the young travelers since they'd arrived at the palace, and the King's eldest son, Reuel, who was the third by that name.

But I would not have you to think that all the rest of the royal princes had been cowards, nor unskilled as soldiers, on the contrary. Much earlier that same day, there had been a hotly contested dispute in the palace over which of the King's sons should be allowed to join in with the regiment. For King Corwan had issued a mandate stating that, at the most, only two of his nine sons could volunteer for the mission, saying it was "unwise" to risk his entire lineage in an untested war. And so, after picking hay straw to decide who should go, the lots of the winners fell to Reuel and Asa, who had both chosen the longer straws.

And thusly, King Corwan ended his speech as the sun rose higher above the hilled plains, thanking the men for their selflessness, to rescue a "dear friend, and a longtime ally." And, that said, it came as only a minor surprise when he announced his intent to join in with the mission, as well, saying in these words, "Therefore, I would be remiss to send my bravest men onward, into such a worthy fight, and not to take my rightful place with them."

From the crowd there came shouts and well wishes for His Majesty's courage. In the end, Corwan announced that "the duty of rule" would be left with the Queen in his absence. This was of course a formality, because the rule of the kingdom always alighted to the Queen during the King's absence, but here too this was met with gracious hoorays.

After his speech, Matilde turned quickly, as if she'd heard a distant signal, or an obvious sound audible only to her.

"It's time," she said, grabbing both young travelers by the hand.

Timothy felt his ears almost burst with a loud ringing, as a bright shot, like a missile of light, went sailing up over the plains, back home to Earth from where it had come.

And like a dream, or something that must be woken from, the King and Queen in all their royal fare, with the citizens of that great city, and generals, and noblemen, in their dapper courtly attire, were vanished. And when they had returned, Timothy and Barbara stood blank faced, in the window room, watching the massive lifelike painting sparkle with the scenes and the stars from that distant world.

Soft ebbs of our own moonlight trickled in through the top gable windows. (For as you should know, though it was still morning in that other world, it was nighttime in our own.)

"Do you think we'll ever go back?" Barbara pondered, with the gleams of far away starlight falling on her face and hair.

Timothy turned to look behind him, out through the tiny passageway and into the attic study beyond, to where his grandmother had disappeared to. His shoulders shrugged, as if he were not so hopeful.

"Maybe, if she ever finds my grandfather... but as it is, she treats me like I'm still this little boy, keeping us here while she's going out to face all sorts of dangers." The tone of his voice heightened to show that he was complaining. "I'm not a little child," he protested.

"Yes, but you are *her* grandchild," Barbara added.

"Still, doesn't mean I'm too young," he repeated. "I could help them find him," he said, placing his hand onto the hilt of his brand new sword. He kept his hand there for a second, trying to imagine how he would fight in battle.

And Barbara stepped in closer, lowering her head to catch his attention.

"But we *are* helping," she replied. "Don't you remember the job she's given us?"

Although Timothy was less than impressed.

"What? To be her postman?... Doesn't seem very important to me."

"Well, not all important things are dangerous. Besides, we're the only ones who can do it, so that makes us important."

"Fine..." Timothy relented, and looked to be softening. "Maybe you're right," he said.

And they went back again to gazing longingly at the moving images of Gleomu in the painting. They saw wide peaceful meadows, and tall ominous mountains, and in one of the corner frames, an elegant city, not nearly as large as the capital city where they'd just come from, but beautiful all the same. (And if you'd looked closely, as closely as they did, you could see people in that pleasant city, moving and going about their days, and once in a while the occasional passing horse cart.)

CHAPTER SIXTEEN
IMPORTANT THINGS

A fter Mrs. Wolcott left the following morning, the next few days were rather uneventful, but only by comparison. For as you might imagine, after living in and truly breathing in the experience of another world, to be resigned to mere correspondence will likely be considered a step backward. And still, perhaps surprisingly, given Timothy's first aversion to his job as an interplanetary postman, the two did their duties with honor, and were very much appreciated for it.

And here was the process as it happened:

Every day, twice a day, for about the space of an hour each time, Barbara would come to visit Wolcott Manor, to help Timothy send and receive their letters; Either from his grandmother and the regiment, who were all steadily riding north, back to the King's palace at Ismere, or vice versa.

The whole matter of interstellar mail carrying was considerably involved. And both messengers agreed, what they thought to be the hardest part of their job was trying to decipher which lake, or hill, or other such landmark they were intended to send the next message to. (Only once, near the beginning, did they guess wrongly, and the bottle came back with an empty letter, and so it had to be resent to the correct coordinates. But that was only once, and after that they both seemed to do much better at finding the appropriate bend in the river, or edge of the forest, and so there was no lasting harm.)

And since nearly all the interest of those days came in form of handwritten letters, if you will allow me, I will recopy those letters here for you, so that you are able to get the full sense of Matilde's journey, from her own words.

Each of her messages came spaced apart, roughly once per day. And in the intermediary time, you should know that Timothy tried very hard to make the most of his days, alone in the house, searching through old chests and hidden rooms, dusting off the pages of age worn books, and finding all sorts of intriguing artifacts. Some of which he'd meant to ask his grandmother if he could keep, including some curious palm-sized dialed instrument that he took for a compass.

And in whatever time remained, he could be seen training, or as Barbara called it "play fighting," with his new sword, on the back hill behind the manor, underneath the shade of an old beech tree.

~ 9th of Kislev, in the 51st year of King Corwan ~

Pleasant greetings, Delany. We are all safe and in good spirits.

Today we rode through to the edge of the low plains, to the village of Loc, where we were welcomed in kindly and a great bonfire was kindled to celebrate our arrival. Which I should expect was at great expense to our hosts, since trees in these plains, we've seen, are not so easy to come by.

At the moment, we are reveling in the late autumn air and are in good company, and these kindnesses have been made all the more sweet, knowing that once we've gone through the pass, past the low Geat Mountains and on toward the rocky barren plains above, it will be pressing travels, and fewer warm greetings till we come to the fort city of Hrim, on the edge of our borders.

Nevertheless, here by the bonfire, at the center of the village, there is dancing, and Corwan is relaying our adventures to date, and mulling over safest routes and passages with the village chief. Now they appear to be speculating, and hearing rumors from the northern county. Just like him, not to rest even when he has a chance for it.

Wishing you could join us, and I know you would be here alongside the bonfire if you were able.

All my affections,

Mattie

~ 10ʰ of Kislev, in the 51ˢᵗ year of King Corwan ~
Our good spirits diminished today.

This morning Corwan made the announcement, while the chilled winds blew through the pass, that there have been rumors of activity on the northern front, and that a few days prior, hunters and pelt traders from the border mountains had come to the village of Loc with stories of possible troop movements within the realm of Ent. None of their claims however could be confirmed by any firsthand knowledge, but the unanticipated displacement of herds has made these rumors more plausible.

Corwan recommended that, considering the necessary dangers of our mission have now changed, and since we have all come as volunteers, that any man who now finds himself fearful should take this opportunity to return back to Ismere, and he's assured them that there will be no disgrace or shame for this action, stating that such men will be counted as messengers, sending back word to the council and generals, and more so, that he would welcome their valor, if war should fall to Ismere.

Dear friend, it pains me to write that you should prepare to welcome so many. Nine men have taken this chance to turn back and to return to the capitol, leaving only thirty-one, plus myself, to continue on across the high plains.

Tonight, the crisp air bites against our cheeks as we huddle here in the shelter of a large crag. We are all cloaked and ready for the winter ahead of us, but say prayers for our bravery as we press on toward Hrim.

Upon reading this letter, Timothy said that he would never have abandoned his grandmother like that, and that those who'd left should be ashamed of themselves. However Barbara, in her way, not wanting to sound at all frightened by their circumstances, said that, "We oughtn't be so quick to judge them." And then added what would turn out to be very fitting, saying that neither of them knew at all what sorts of armies one might face, out there in that other world.

~ 11th of Kislev, in the 51ˢᵗ year of King Corwan ~

Another day in this barren waste. Vivid green heath and the sun obscured by fogs and clouds that rain down upon us, and these giant boulders spread throughout the expanding landscape.

And the sun, when it is bright, comes in a way that you might imagine this laboring fog might end, but it never does. And it brings back, when it comes again, a more biting dampness, and the winter's frost in the wind.

The sun looks to be fully setting soon. We've made a camp at the basin of a low point between two hills, to escape the wind.

~12ᵗʰ of Kislev, in the 51ˢᵗ year of King Corwan ~

I can only imagine these plains to be a beautiful place during the summers, though it looks like we have come upon them in their foul season.

Today we found a small clean pool, to fill our containers with and to water the horses.

~13ᵗʰ of Kislev, in the 51ˢᵗ year of King Corwan ~

This morning we awoke with a thin line of frost over our blankets, and in the strands of our hair. My fingers are beginning to stiffen, making it difficult to write a proper letter.

[After this point Matilde's hand appeared to have been shivering, and so the last few lines were hardly discernible at all, except for the word "**ICE**", which was written in very bold script.]

~14ᵗʰ of Kislev, in the 51ˢᵗ year of King Corwan ~

I'd almost thought this desolate expanse would have gone on forever, but tonight we've finally come to Hrim. We'd arrived a full hour after sunset, and rode along, our path obscured in the darkened plains. Yet, no one would bear speak of setting camp, for on ahead we saw the faint glow of distant lights, of the outpost city and its watchtower, like a beacon of promise in this frigid hardened land.

In an instant, we were all of us settled around the warm hearth, in a tall and long stretched wooden lodge. And as the fire lapped at our icy hands and faces, our spirits returned to us, and a deeper laughter, of the sort that hides dormant inside battered and wearied bodies, that joyfulness began to melt and flow from our souls and limbs. It is good to be warmed again.

As you might like to know, during these few days when Barbara and Timothy had been engaged in their duties as postmen, Timothy had kept very well fed. So much, that he would sometimes only eat because it was time for it, and not for any real need, or lack: Taking his opportunity to devour each of his grandmother's left over tart pastries, and whole custards, washing them down with glasses of milk left to him every morning by the milkman who'd still kept a regular route in Mayfield.

But as for Barbara, she had not been so fortunate, and was on to her third day of clumpy porridge fed to her in the school's dining commons. Everyone, left abandoned on the grounds that summer, agreed that it was some sort of hardly edible torture, made from lentils, or green soup peas, or some pureed mix of the other horrid awful food left to the "orphans" at Mayfield. And truly, Barbara had fully begun to pity herself, until she read the last and final message sent back to them from the fort city of Hrim.

It was scorched, as if by fire, and not even rolled into its customary greenish bottle, but came floating down through the air and landed on the window room floor. This letter bore only one word, though that in itself was enough, and even more than Barbara thought she might be able to bear reading without sudden tears.

ATTACK......

The word was scrawled largely across the page, and as Timothy was certainly convinced, was not even in his grandmother's own handwriting.

"We have to do something," Timothy said, raising his voice. However, Barbara was not so hot headed as her friend, and thought within herself that both she and Timothy were, neither of them, strong enough to do any real good.

"And what could we do?" she retorted.

"Oh, I don't know," he said, motioning his open hand toward the glowing painting, and the images of that distant, unfamiliar, and now obviously dangerous new world.

"...But something."

CHAPTER SEVENTEEN
A DECISION

✦

A mighty uproar ran through the council, calling for greater military intervention, anything at all that could be done to save the King, the royal princes, and those valiant men who'd offered themselves for this horrific mission.

There was chaotic yelling and loud voices. Barbara and Timothy stood in the center of it all, after retelling to the council the story of how this final letter had come to them, and after reading aloud its single worded message.

One man stood up to remark that their kingdom's friendship with Earth had cost them more than it was worth. Though, thankfully no one gave his accusation much credence, and afterward another of the noblemen declared that now the time had finally come to use the light for its intended purpose, to transport reinforcements.

Howbeit, Queen Delany, who was sovereign in her husband's absence, declared that she would by no means disobey the King's edict, even now. (Which states that every native born citizen of their world shall be forbidden from light travel, including the King himself.) And furthermore, in this specific instance the Queen also refused to use the light for herself, to leave her kingdom uncared for during such a time of crisis.

And so, it would seem there was nothing else to be done, but to deploy a band of soldiers as a search party, and to send messengers to the outlying northern settlements, and to wait and hope for the King's good return, or for word of his safety, or otherwise.

Their soup of chilled strawberries and currants, in the emptied banquet hall, would have delighted even the most soured expression, but that evening it did little to comfort their sadness, or to lift their sense of hopelessness.

Timothy and Barbara sat side-by-side, enjoying plush velvety chairs, and all the courtly delicacies that the palace could afford them: But this did little, very little, to enliven their spirits. After all, what good is a king's banquet when there is no king? When the ones you care for are put so dearly into harm's way? In moments like those, a bowl of strawberry and currant soup does little good. In fact, it will most often ferment with sadness, and taste bitter in your mouth. (And if I might place a guess at the reason for this, I would say it is because heavy feelings: such as sadness, bitterness, or guilt, leave no room for the other senses, and will weigh down into the dust even the best of niceties.)

After a long passing silence, Timothy finally spoke up, setting his silver engraved spoon on the table.

"You can stay if you'd like, but I'm going to find her."

Barbara nearly spit out her soup. "The King and thirty men couldn't even stand up to them, and survive. What good are you going to do?"

"Maybe I'll catch them by surprise," he said, turning in his chair to face hers, and leaning his elbow atop the table.

"*Maybe* you'll get yourself killed," she responded, looking rather cross.

"Hey now, just because you're too frightened to go, doesn't mean that I have to be. I can defend myself," he said, placing a hand on the emerald green and golden hilt of his new sword.

But Barbara just rolled her eyes and scoffed, "And just because you've got a sword," she said, folding her arms, "...that doesn't make you knight."

Timothy pushed away from the banquet table, and stood up. "No... but neither does staying here."

And he stormed out of the room, his footsteps echoing in her ears as he left.

And she continued to hear those last words and footsteps, mingled with her own, as she made her way to Timothy's quarters that evening. Though her steps, at the present, had made a much more firm and resounding tone than they'd usually had, for she had just swapped her old laced boots for a newer fur lined pair that she'd found tucked away in her ample palace

81

closet. Imagining that no one would ever mind her enjoying such a stylish and cozy pair, considering the fact that she, of course, was counted as an honored guest there at palace, and that those sorts of boots would be the exact type she might have been given anyhow, that is if anyone there had known the manner of dangerous, and somewhat foolishly heroic plans that they had decided upon that evening, but thankfully no one had.

She arrived at his door, bit down her top lip, and knocked forcefully.

"Who's there?"

"It's me, Barbara."

"What do you want, Cholley? Come to try to talk me out of it, are you?" he said rudely through the door, so that she nearly changed her mind.

But from that she stopped herself, for she knew that what she had wanted most of all at the moment was to help rescue Mrs. Wolcott, and if she would have to put up with her rude grandson's behavior in the process, then, as much as necessary, she would endure, if that meant saving that dear old woman's life.

"Noo..." she answered back, slightly mocking him. "I *want* to help."

And before she knew quite what was happening, the door swung open and Timothy's hand was stuck out to her, offering her some mess of wadded puffy fabric mixed with animal skins.

"What's this?" she asked, rightfully.

"Silly, it's your coat," Timothy replied.

And then added, slightly enjoying himself, for the adventure of it all, and dramatically overemphasizing every word, "It's sure to be very... very cold."

CHAPTER EIGHTEEN

THE JOURNEY BEGINS

Their boots crunched on the cold frozen grassy tundra, like they were walking on fields of crystalized rock candies. Puffs of white misty breaths went up around their faces.

All the small bluffs, hills, and rocky icy green plains looked so unsettlingly the same. In fact, so much so, that they had never known for sure whether or not they weren't actually blindly traveling around in circles. Except for this, that Timothy felt absolutely certain his new intricate compass, that he'd found hidden away in one of the dusty rooms of the Wolcott Manor, had been leading them due north since they'd landed on the plains that morning.

But by now the sun was starting to settle lower on the horizon, and they were still desperately lost, with a full week's time left before they were both to be "reflected back to Earth", as his grandmother would call it. Which unfortunately was just enough time to run them dangerously close to the end of their food and water rations, but would certainly allow them more than enough time to freeze to death, as Barbara had pointed out, somewhat untactfully, during a particularly frigid and blustery portion of the day. And almost when Barbara had begun to strike up her resolve, to insist that they had better find a spot to make camp for the night, the wind blew one last hard gust from what they had assumed to be the northeast.

"I say," Timothy proclaimed, laughing as he spoke. "Do you smell that?"

Barbara's nose crinkled.

"Smoke?" she said, as if questioning her senses.

"Jolly right," he smiled. "And fire, and warmth, and people."

And by two of those three accounts, Timothy was completely accurate, and should be credited for it. Howbeit, when they'd finally arrived, in the cold and looming dusk, to their horror they found the fort city of Hrim entirely decimated, burned with fire. Its buildings were left smoldering or shattered into pieces, only one wall of one small general's quarters had remained standing, and in the dark, with numb fingers, Timothy was able to get a fire going with the embers and broken half-burned pieces of old buildings. They wrapped up tightly in their coats, and made beds of scorched blankets.

More and more, the cloudy and ash filled darkness began to descend upon that sieged and wasted city, too black to see anything of the full devastation before nightfall. And so they huddled in their smokey beds, faces laid down in soot and charred dust; Hoping that, whatever horrible enemy had raged through the outpost city, it would not see their campfire light that night, burning like a beacon across those icy fields, which they'd needed for warmth, and that it, or they, would not come back to attack them in their sleep.

And that night, Barbara slept holding on tightly to a small red-handled, child-sized dagger they'd found back in Mayfield. This slight comfort helped her to finally rest her eyes, but she could not sleep soundly. In the early morning hours, before dawn, the fire settled and the air grew damp like melted snow; It was spectacularly uncomfortable, but this was not a mission for comfort. Both Timothy and Barbara knew this quite well. This was a mission for bravery, or nothing at all.

CHAPTER NINETEEN

THE RUINS

✦

As brutal as the destruction of Hrim had seemed in the late evening, when the edges of darkness hid most of the ruins from their plain sight, by the time the sun had finally risen and several early fog clouds had lifted they could at last see the utter wastedness of it.

And this is what they saw: Huge smoldering projectiles dotted throughout the city, like massive clumps of tar balled up with rocks, that had been showered across the battered landscape. Each of these balls of tar and stone seemed to have been nearly eight feet tall, at one time, but had been smushed upon impact to be wider around the center now. (Very similar in shape to how flying saucers were made to look like in early black and white cinema, only these projectiles reeked of burning oily tar, with clouds of dense cruel smoke billowing off of them.

"Looks like catapults to me," Timothy mentioned, poking at a massive black blob with what had been the lower portion of a chair.

They were both standing within the remains of what had once been a supply station. Albeit, the only reason how that could be known at all was because scattered around their feet lay the wreckage of charred bags of grain and completely disintegrated pieces of fruit barrels and wine kegs. The only bits of food left preserved were some jarred and bottled items that hadn't been smashed open, but none of which looked appetizing, their glass outsides burnt black in the fire, so that you could not distinguish a jar of pickled ham from a jar of pickles.

But while they stood there examining the burning tar balls, Barbara, who'd been so overly preoccupied with her course work during the previous term, knew from an introductory study of physics what great force would be needed to move such a sea of heavy ammunition, like these, that had been fired out over the city's ruins. Not to mention the strength it might take to move such enormous catapults, ones that would be required to launch blob missiles of this size. And from where would they have come? Who knows how far an enemy like this would have needed to travel, and through this nearly frozen wasteland.

"You know," Barbara said, picking up another charred stick to begin her own investigation. "They would need whole fields of horses to even budge these tar boulders." Which seemed a good enough name as any to call them. And Barbara, perhaps more than usual, at this moment wished to be thought of as helpful, and smart, knowing that at the present she'd not been overly helpful since they'd arrived. For after all, it was Timothy who'd brought a compass, and discovered the ruined city, and Timothy who'd built them a fire the night before to keep them warm. That is not to say, that in her heart she hadn't only wanted to rescue Mrs.

Wolcott, no matter the cost, but that she'd also hoped not to be too babied in the process.

Still, her male cohort was now feeling incredibly boyish, and would not even grant her that simple courtesy.

"Who says they'd used horses?" Timothy intruded.

Barbara looked up at him hoarsely. "Well, what else would they have used?" she questioned.

"Who knows... elephants maybe," he said, as if being actually serious.

She could barely refrain herself, and nearly laughed at him.

"Elephants?!" she exclaimed, and then she rested from her own examination of the tar boulder to point out the obvious.

"Where would *anyone* get elephants in a place like this?"

"How should I know?" he replied.

And Timothy now left his boulder to see if there wasn't any lick of food strewn around that was worth saving.

"Doesn't mean it didn't happen though... Hannibal did the same thing when he attacked the Romans, brought elephants down through the mountains," he explained, while also beginning to stow what might have been jars of radishes into his side satchel for the journey.

And as you will come to know, Barbara had always hated thinking that she was not being taken seriously. And so she turned quickly, using her black tar-tipped prodding stick she'd still held in her hand as a means to visualize her point.

"Let's have at it then," she said, motioning out toward the open fields where the catapult shots were undoubtedly fired from. "Whatever animals they've used, there's got to be tracks of them out in that field, and I bet, if we follow them, they'll lead us straight to your grandmother."

"That's the stuff, Cholley," Timothy exclaimed. "I knew you'd come in handy."

It was a nice enough compliment, but only because he'd meant it sincerely. However, Barbara still could not avoid rolling her eyes back ever so slightly, thinking to herself, *"What an awfully boyish way to give a compliment."*

"Race you," he yelled back, already several steps ahead.

And the two went rushing off away, out of the ruins, toward the open fields under the gaze of an ominous high mountain range. Timothy sprinted through the low grass and peat, but he was not yet accustomed to running with a sword at his side, so that Barbara soon passed him up.

"No fair," he shouted. "I can't r-AHH!"

Flat on his face, and the contents of his satchel went spilling over the hillside.

He had begun to say, "I can't run like this," but had tripped so suddenly, and unexpectedly, that his words came out as a yelp. His hands scuffed and new winter coat dirtied, but at least, he thought, he had not been cut by his own sword, something not at all impressive for a prince to do.

"Are you hurt?" Barbara called, speeding back to help him off the ground.

"I'm fine... not hurt at all, just this blasted hole here," he said, looking down at where he had fallen.

"What an odd shape?" Barbara noticed, mostly speaking aloud to collect her thoughts.

"That's what I thought," Timothy spoke up, and showing his skills of observation once again, said, "You'd expect a hole to be dug out, like with a spade, but this one looks like it's been stamped, or pressed into the ground, like-"

"Like a footprint," Barbara interrupted, looking pale white.

"Exactly," he said excitedly, but then quickly caught his senses, seeing how distraught Barbara now looked to be.

"Yes..." he said, repeating this truth. "Exactly like a footprint."

CHAPTER TWENTY
A BIG PROBLEM
✦

G iants.

Giant footsteps speckled across the rolling low hills. Everywhere imprints of horridly mammoth giant boots and shoeless giant feet (roughly a meter and a half long, and a half a meter wide).

There was no denying it. An army of giants had laid siege to the city of Hrim, and had stolen away, or worse, killed, Mrs. Matilde Wolcott, the Queen of Earth. But that had not meant that Barbara had not wished to deny it, even forgoing her better judgement, she tried to make the point that all they knew were the sizes of their footprints, and who's to say that these enemy soldiers had not been moderately averaged sized men, with only disproportionately giant sized feet.

However, Timothy had said not very tactfully, but rightly in this case, that that was impossible, and that they should call giants what they are, or else they will never be able to defeat them when the time comes.

But this had not been the sort of encouragement Barbara had hoped for, and so they walked on in silence, following a horde of crevassed footprints and canyonous ruts from the catapult wheels. These tracks slowly carrying them further and further from the ashes of Hrim, toward the steep and craggy mountain faces ahead of them.

And as Timothy was still in the process of experimenting, deciding whether or not he could clear the length of an entire giant's stride, with the added weight of his sword and satchel, he said these words (not meaning to sound uninviting, but that's how it appeared):

"You don't have to come along, you know," he said, readying himself for another jump.

"Ah!" Barbara's mouth dropped open in disgust. "And you'd just leave me there in that ash heap, I bet," she said, pointing back toward the tiny dot of smoke on the horizon that they'd been making good distance from all morning.

Timothy stopped himself before he could jump again, turning back toward his new friend. "And what, you'd rather face up against giants with me?" He placed a hand on the hilt of his newfangled emerald sword, as if that were his natural stance now.

Jagged pointed rocks and rings of clouds near the peaks of the range, Barbara's eyes took in the seemingly insurmountable peril of it all, and tried diligently to make herself less scared than she actually was.

"Well, no..." she said. "I'd rather not do either of those."

She ran her fingers through her straight hair, as she will do sometimes to help gather her thoughts.

"But I've decided to be brave, for your grandmother's sake."

"And I'm sure she'd be proud of you," Timothy answered back, sincerely.

This so surprised Barbara that she smiled, as if almost by reflex. Perhaps, her traveling companion, who'd been rushing on ahead of her, and who'd been not so entirely considerate as she would have liked, ever since their very first late night meeting in the attic study, perhaps now he'd finally prove to be a gentleman.

But these hopes, as decent as they were, were suddenly crushed to pieces when Timothy shot back a response, as if not even realizing the compliment he'd given.

"So we should be going then, right?"

And with that he turned again, following those giants' footprints, not even waiting for her, or letting Barbara first respond to what she was nearly certain may have been an actual question.

The sun had not yet burned through the high fog that morning, by the time the two came to the foot of those spindling mountains, overlooking the northern edge of the kingdom. There at the base of the mountain range the overwhelming mass of the giant army's footsteps appeared to have turned and headed due south, toward the heart of Gleomu.

(It might serve well here to point out that one of the downfalls, historically, for any giant army has been that in an open plain, such as this was, they are almost certainly chronically incapable of dealing a surprise attack, being seen hours and hours beforehand by any half-decent watchman. And this is nearly always the case, and a good enough reason why you have not heard tell of very many giant victories in recent years, expect for this one provision to the rule: Which states that if a giant army can manage to use a range of mountains as a means of camouflage, then they might be able to handily overcome their disadvantageous heredity.)

"Looks like they're not done fighting, either," Barbara noticed, seeing their tracks leading away from them, toward the capital city.

"Except for this bigger one here," Timothy said, and pointed to a larger set of prints, even by giant standards, that had separated itself from the rest of the army, and had gone stomping onward toward the base of the mountain. These humungous steps made a dead stop at a steep rock face, and then turned again, traveling along the edge of the range to join in once more with the other giant steps, and were after which mingled in with the rest of the tracks and were lost for good.

"That's odd," Barbara's nose wrinkled as she said it.

She had been standing directly inside one of the large giant's massive tracks, the imprint of it was unconscionably deep, and she imagined the ferocious weight needed to make such cavernous steps, and she felt the most noticeably painful sense of fear that she'd had since arriving for their rescue mission, and she hoped to never have to encounter, face-to-face, such a monstrous giant within her lifetime.

But Timothy spoke up, soon stirring her from this awful daydream.

"That's right, it is odd," Timothy replied, rubbing his thumb and forefinger along the edge of his jawline (as he'll sometimes do to help collect his thoughts).

"Fowl luck we're not giants as well, or else we'd know what was so interesting about this ugly mountain," he said.

And it was just then that something peculiar had happened, something that would redirect the course of their adventures, as if by chance, or otherwise. From out of the low ceiling-like mist of white fog above them, they heard the shriek of a bird of prey (and as for the exact species, well neither two travelers at that time would have known enough of Ornithology, which is the study of birds, to have been able to give a name to it, but I can tell you that it was a falcon, although a much larger breed of falcon than we tend to have on earth). It circled above for a few seconds, before landing upon a high ledge, on a stack of square rocks that appeared to have been chiseled, and put into place quite intentionally. However, it was the type of thing one might never have notice on one's own, not without a bird to land upon it.

"Is that a stone column?" Timothy said peculiarly.

"If it is, then those rocks next to it must be a column as well," Barbara answered.

"And look there," he said again, pointing across to the other side of the narrow and sharp ravine, in which they now stood at the entrance to.

The pair had come a long way from Hrim, and were now looking forward into a cleft in the mountain, which they could see as a dead-ended alleyway with high steep walls, that helpfully blocked some of the cold wind that blew at them from the open plain. But if you were to get a bird's-eye view, in this case, from atop either of those stone columns, you would see it as a deep and dangerous rocky chasm.

And this is what Timothy had seen when he'd somewhat shouted, saying, "And look there", it was a second set of pillars, at roughly the same height, set on an opposite ledge, almost mirrored across the chasm.

"More pillars?" she said aloud, and then she realized it. "You don't think this used to be a rope bridge, above us?"

"What else *could* it be," Timothy said smiling, and perhaps too overly proud of his own keen sense of observation, so that he'd not noticed Barbara's contributions.

"And where there are bridges," he said, allowing for a dramatic pause, "...there are roads."

And Timothy was most excited about this fact, until Barbara had made a very simple observation that he indeed might have overlooked.

"So..." she said, staring at a very sillily excited Timothy Hayfield. "How do you suppose we get up there then?"

This caused Timothy, who had never fancied heights all that dearly, to suddenly realize their predicament, and as he grew more fearful all the color seemed to disappear from his face.

"Oh, right," he said.

In his fear, he gulped a distinguishably loud gulp of chilled air: That blew in across the cold hard plains and into their steeply walled precipice, where they now stood, left to wonder and examine this new, previously unimagined danger.

CHAPTER TWENTY-ONE

A NEW ROAD

✦

B arbara, and Timothy both, had been very proud of *their* idea: Stating that since this was a road, or had been at one time, that therefore one side must lead upward, higher into the mountains, and that meant the other side must have a lower entrance that they might get to.

And again, they were both very proud of their cleverness, as they found that same entrance for the mountain road only a half a mile's walk from their missing bridge. And again, as they were choosing their steps over the empty paving stones on that ancient trail, but this same pride, in these happy discoveries, quickly diminished, once they saw just how far a distance that missing footbridge had spread across the open ravine.

"How do we even know there's anything across there?" Timothy said, directing his hand out toward the other ledge, and letting his eyes follow down the steep walls to the bottom.

"Oh, don't start."

Barbara looked stern. And slightly, maybe deep down, so that even she did not fully realize her own emotions, she found it comforting for once to be the brave one in this circumstance.

This vacuous, awful cut in the mountain face before them, where the ancient rope bridge had once hung between the four pillars, it seemed like the worst leap imaginable. Thoughts of falling swirled inside Timothy's head; And bits of that same fear he swallowed, and those made their way sinking down into his stomach, filling it with nerves, which in the end trickled into his legs, making them of no use at all.

"I'm not so sure about this," he said, as though breathing in his words at the end.

And afterward, Timothy had finally got the courage to express what he'd been feeling for some time.

"How do we even know the giants took her this way?"

Barbara's eyes opened wide to give a well deserved scowl. "We don't," she answered quickly. "And we can't, not unless we make it over there," she continued, motioning her hand out across that despicable hole.

However, here, Timothy was quick to say that, "No one could ever jump that far."

But to that Barbara answered him, saying they didn't have any choice, and that his grandmother needed them to be brave, at least a little, and she assured him they could make the leap, though they would need a full speed running start at it.

Timothy looked, once more, over the gaping crevasse.

"Are you serious?" he spoke, mostly to himself.

"Watch me," Barbara answered, wiping her hair from her face.

She hurled her pack with all her strength, and it landed safely, in a puff cloud of gravel dust.

"At least something can make the distance," she thought.

And then Barbara did what had seemed impossible, and in a normal circumstance she would have never worked up the courage enough to take such a leap, but she knew what not jumping would mean; And to a greater degree, she had absolutely abhorred any thought that she were a coward, and she wanted to settle this notion once and for all, proving she would be worth her salt on this trip, and able to be brave on her own.

Twenty paces back would do it, she thought to herself, making sure her coat was buttoned and shoelaces tucked in. Nothing could snag, or trip her up. There was no retrying something like this; Either she made it soundly to the other side, or else she'd grievously misjudged her abilities and there was no coming back.

"Tim?"

She did not give him time to answer.

"If you die here, do you die for real?" she was quite a distance down the road, and had to speak this more loudly than I'd imagine any normal person would have wanted to.

"Let's just say you do," Timothy answered. It was not at all comforting, but honest.

"Now!" she yelled within her head.

And before she could know why, she was sprinting: Faster, faster, being careful to keep her footing on the uneven stones. The last step, with all her resolve, like a bird across the canyon, and her toes just reaching the other side. For a split second she teetered, toes on the ledge, heels out over the empty nothingness. Then the gravel gave way, falling.

"Ahh!"

She just managed to catch the ledge with her arms, and her upper torso, but her lower half dangled off the edge. No foothold, nothing but loose coarse sand to grab onto.

"Help! Timothy!" she screamed, with all she could pull from her lungs. There was no cry more terrible.

Clunk.

A sword clanked over her head, and a satchel with a heavy coat tied around the strap. The ground beneath her hands began to pull from her grasp.

"Hurry! Hurry!" she yelled.

"I'm coming," shouted a voice from far behind her, but rushing closer.

Footsteps.

Faster, faster, faster.

A cry of desperation as he leapt from the other side and landed, rolling on the dirt and being bruised across the cobble stone. And a dirtied hand with blood on the knuckles reached out, while supporting against the old pillar, and helped to pull Barbara to safety.

The two sat dumbfounded, looking out over the edge where they had so nearly lost their lives.

"Thank you," Barbara sighed earnestly.

"You almost had it," he let out, giving a pat on her back, like he'd been completely unstartled the entire time, which made Barbara altogether grateful and painfully infuriated, all at the same time.

"Oh look, horse tracks," Timothy said, breathing heavy, peering over his shoulder at the mountain road, which continued on behind them.

CHAPTER TWENTY-TWO
THE MOUNTAINS

A single imprint of something that might have been his grandmother's boot print. Of course, given the general uniform nature of boot prints, it could have come from anyone. Yet, in their hearts, they were sure of it, that that massive unearthly-sized giant must have carried Mrs. Wolcott away, captive from the burned city of Hrim, and had delivered her to some mysterious horse rider. All the slimly discernible facts seemed to point to only one conclusion: The Queen of Earth would be found somewhere within the belly of those ominous and gnarled black mountains.

It was barely enough to raise any hope, but what other choice had they, so that under those presumptions they continued, following the mysterious horseman's tracks, knowing that they could never safely return the way they had come, for it was only by an undeniable miracle that they'd even both survived thus far.

This mangled highway curved and skewed along the edge of many more such deadly cliffs. On the road, many of the original paving stones had dislodged overtime, and portions of the trail were washed away, leaving only thin strips of loose gravel, falling off into voids of black nothing, or worse, sharp and jagged pits.

However, amazingly, the mysterious horseman was somehow able to maneuver across even the thinnest slivers of trail, and continue on, into the misty dark grey and black clouded spiraling range.

Sunlight began to fail them, and around them it grew more difficult to tell the exact reason for this. Could it be that the ceiling of fog and clouds overhead had finally surrounded them? Or had the sun grown more frightened of these grotesque peaks, and had refused to share its light with them?

Icy vapors began to solidify around them, and Barbara had begun to think it wise to have already used up the last drops in her water container, before it froze up for good.

Yet, before the light had drifted away completely, their path widened into a sheerly walled canyon, and they made camp by a swelling waterfall. The ground was scattered with heavy rocks, but they were able to clear enough away, to make for a softer sandy bed, and with a little hunting they were able to find some firewood along a nearby steep hillside, some of which appeared at have already been burned. And all night long the flickers of their campfire would reflect off the waterfall, moving in and out like a breath through the cascading waters, and obscured at times by the rising mist.

In the morning, very stiff and irritable, and with grumbling stomachs, Timothy and Barbara awoke to realize for themselves this simple truth: that a camp made near a waterfall makes for a very soggy bedroll. During the night their fire had burned away, little by little, and now all their feet and hands felt like icicles, and Barbara was sincerely aware her nose had never been so cold, and she rubbed it ferociously with the palm of her hand to try to warm it.

But one good thing about a damp bed is that you will waste no time in getting up, and so Timothy began to scour through his satchel in search of those mysterious jars of food he'd rescued from the ashes of Hrim. They opened a few of these scorched black mystery containers and found one of them to be a jar of pickled eggs, and the other a jar of soured potatoes. (And as much as it may surprise you to hear told about, both Timothy and Barbara eventually agreed that the pickled eggs were actually quite good, and that they had just needed salt. Which would be scarcely hard to come by during their travels, but still they didn't see any harm in wishing for it.)

"Even the embers are freezing," Timothy moaned, prodding through the coals to see if any would reignite.

He'd been crouching with his back to the waterfall, and had been also in a rather foul mood, because his water ration had frozen shut during the middle of the night, and now he was keeping it tucked into his jacket pocket to thaw, but that only made him all the more cold, and crankier still.

Barbara was, as well, crouching down beside the ashes of their paltry fire, examining it to see if she could be of any help, but had all of a sudden, and curiously, stood up, with the most flustered appearance burned upon her face.

"Timothy, Timothy..." she was saying his name over and over again, until he'd finally given her his attention.

"What?" he said, not looking up, still staring at the gone out coals.

Her voice shook slightly, "You know that reflection in the waterfall... [not giving him time to answer], well I don't think it's a real one." (And she was speaking of course about the flickering reflection of their campfire in the midst of the waterfall, that had burned steadily all through the night.)

"No?" he questioned, looking up at Barbara, who was now beginning to show her real fear.

"What if there's someone else here?" she whispered, not taking her eyes away from that puzzling flame.

And with these hushed words, Timothy could now see the full extent of his traveling companion's fright. Though, being contrary to her, he wanted to show himself to be completely unfrightened, thinking it brave, or heroic, to do so. So that, in like manner he arose, falsely confident, up from his poor job tending their own sickly campfire, and he yelled out to whatever stranger was there tending to his own fire, there through the blanketed waterfall. However, this was of course horridly foolish of him.

He took a half-step forward, yelling, "Hey, you there?"

Vanished, the fire was snuffed out completely. Too quickly to have been burning wood or charcoal, like the flame on a gas burning stove top, which can be outed suddenly, like it had never burned at all.

Rustling echoed out, as if from the mouth of a cave, and a giant figure moved behind the veiled water like a shadow. Rocks toppled, thrashed about by something very massive and certainly terrifying. Whatever had lain behind that misty water was something instantly known to be unfriendly, and Timothy felt now perhaps the most foolish and brazen as he'd ever felt in his whole life, and rightfully so.

The breadth of those falls parted through the center, and that something, that had lain in secret now emerged, dark and evil black-green.

CHAPTER TWENTY-THREE

BEASTS

A dragon.

If you've never before seen a dragon, then you will not begin to know how to imagine such a monster. (And by this I mean a real dragon, not those passive imitations you might find in a Hollywood matinee.)

Real dragons are slithering and lightning fast as serpents, with putrid tar black smoke in their nostrils, and not those fairy wings over their backs, but dagger-sharp black bat-like wings, that stretch out almost infinitely to either side. And to this you may begin to say, 'Well wait, that was the sort of thing I'd imagined all along.' Which may be a partial truth, but trust me when I say that, whatever thoughts you may have held regarding dragons, if you have not seen a real one, in the flesh, with its iron-like scales, then I assure you, the creature of your own imagining will be in no part as wild or as beastly as the true monster.

And so, for that reason, it should be no wonder why our forefathers, from every corner of our world, had feared them as they did, each framing them into their own myths and legends, even long after their armies and knights had, with much sacrifice, finally slain the last of them, and had ridded them from our world altogether. But not from all worlds.

The beast, as tall as a spire, leapt through the air, out from his craggy lair, splitting the cascading falls in half. Boiling hot mist struck off its wings. Its mouth opened with a set of double rowed teeth, and let out a shrill and deathly biting cry. A flash of incendiary flames burnt out its throat. Wings beat slowly and forcefully, to keep it above the icy pool at the base of the falls. Neck lurching, it glared, voided dark eyes, at the children.

Timothy drew his sword, and rushed up to stand between Barbara and the monstrous dragon. With one hand brandishing his emerald and silvery sword, and with the other bracing, trying to keep Barbara back behind him, or to be whatever barrier he could between her and the beast.

These were just the sorts of things he'd dreamt about several nights before, laying wrapped up safely in his comfortable palace bed, and there, with his new sword propped upon a cushy feather pillow. Except that, in his imaginations that night, those monsters, and beasts, and dragons he'd vested and slain were, all of them, much more tame and simple, and he himself had been many times more valiant and strong.

However, those elusive dreams were not this present true reality. And like with most things one might envision, as with this: It is that when the true monsters come, they are often more wild and more savage than our thoughts of them. Being as it is, that imaginary dragons are most always easily slain.

The monster cried again with a fire in its voice. It mounted upward, beating its sharpened wings, the tips of which spread out, filling to the edges of the canyon where they'd made their camp in the night before.

"Run," Timothy said turning to her. "I'll stay here, and fend him off."

But Barbara could not bear the thought.

"No!" she answered loudly.

And reaching into her pack she drew out her own dagger, and she held up her knife to the beast, then came to stand alongside her partner, and brushed the hair from her eyes, catching a glance at Timothy. By a look, the two knew instantly that whatever fight they might make now would be insignificant, but that it would be wrong not to at least try.

Flushes of wind, both icy and steaming hot, flew through the canyon, as the creature beat its wings, mixing with the mist from the waterfall. Its chest began to swell, as if building a fire within itself. It screamed with all violence, preparing to lunged at the children. But, at the same time, there was another scream, seemingly just as violent, from high atop the canyon ledge.

It was a man. A fearless knight with long raven black hair and beard, he was leaping from off the high canyon wall, a long sword clenched tightly in his fists, and speeding through the expanse, over the waterfall's edge and the icy pool, as if arriving from a dead sprint.

He soared through the air, over the body of the beast, and in the last second spun his sword, and pointing it downward, gripped in both hands, he drove its razor sharp blade through the top of the vile creature's skull.

In the blink of an eye, the dragon's body was lifeless. Its wings folded under, and both the beast and its vanquisher fell with an uncontrollable force into the shallow pool at the base of the falls. A blast of flash boiled water exploded upwards out of the canyon, and rained down like a hot geyser.

A very audible sigh of relief left Timothy's lips. They were saved. And just as he was realizing that the knight had not yet come up for air, out upon the rocky bank of the pool emerged a recently familiar face, water dripping off the chin of his beard, and some of it puddled in the cuffs of his pant legs. It was Asa, the King's son.

He wiped the wet hair away from his face.

"What? No thank you?" he said, as if joking to himself.

For the children had been caught speechless, but this only lasted for a moment. Soon they were congratulating Asa, thanking him profusely for rescuing them; And "so heroically," as Barbara began to say (and what became more frequent than Timothy eventually cared for).

The majority of the dragon's carcass had fallen below the surface of the water, but its grotesque, charcoal black and greenish head, and a quarter portion of its neck had fallen onto the bank of that small pool. With all his strength Asa heaved his sword out of the creature. And then, seeing Timothy's noticeably poorly unlit fire, he told them to stand aside as he pressed his hefty leather boots against a set of folds on the dragon's neck, and with that, one final funnel of flames scorched out of the beast's open mouth, setting ablaze the coals and any damp firewood that had remained unburned.

As the fire kindled, they became warm again, and with that, Timothy was quite sure this was going to be a much better adventure, from now on. Although, he'd been fairly convinced that he hadn't needed any real help with starting a fire.

CHAPTER TWENTY-FOUR
A STORY

✦

"The watchmen had heard the noise of an army in the open field, and had seen torchlight off in the distance, on the night before the attack, but nothing could have prepared us for the dawn, and an army of a thousand giants."

Asa was recounting his story of the attack on Hrim, while leading them on a single filed march, further up into the clouded, foreboding mountains, and he continued:

"Giants, on their own, are menacing and formidable in battle, but to our benefit have been historically unimaginative... not unintelligent; But better put, as a culture, giants do not tend to share well amongst themselves, and so while you may have several bright or prominent giants within a generation, very often those giant leaders will die off, or will be viciously murdered, taking their discoveries with them. And therefore, leaving each newer generation with only the basest forms of government and rudimentary tools.

And so you can imagine our utter shock and horror, to awake to find a sea of enormous catapults and a more than sufficient army. When all they've ever had, in recent centuries, were bands of lawless giants, with clubs and blunted amateurish swords."

"Do you think someone was helping them, then?" Barbara interjected, as the three were making their way along a narrow winding trail, being sure to stay at all times several paces away from the deadly cliff's ledge to their left, away from that haunting drop into the murky chasm below.

Timothy had been taking a gulp from his water container, that was by now thawed completely, when he suddenly had an idea mid-drink.

"Ooh," he gargled. And then skimming away the excess water droplets from his chin and lips, he said more clearly, "Like maybe this mysterious horseman."

Asa smiled a deep bearded grin. "Ha," he laughed. "Well done, but you tend to ruin a story when you spoil its ending like that," he said, as if falsely stern.

And to that the children apologized directly, and asked him to continue. However their guide had not been so easily offended, and was actually quite impressed by their ability to reason, and so he never acknowledged their apologies, but continued on.

"Nearly an hour after sunrise, a younger giant, a scout, came to the gate to warn us that Hrim would be 'desolate and burned with a thousand fires', to quote his words exactly, if we did not immediately deliver to them the Queen of Earth. And they launched a warning shot into the center square of the city to demonstrate their severity."

"And... did you hand her over?" Timothy interrupted, beginning to sound offended for his grandmother's sake, and for her safety.

"Was not necessary," Asa answered back, and Barbara saw his face as he said this, and thought that this had not been his first choice either.

"Her Majesty volunteered herself," Asa continued. "And she would not be swayed. She said that, 'This was the clearest route to finding her husband, and if it would need to be by the hands of giants, then that was what was required.' "

"Oh, I can't imagine," Barbara said aloud, as she stepped over a patch of loose gravel, along the thin and narrowing foot trail.

"Yes, well, our King knew full well that even that would not be enough to appease them, and that giants do not very often keep true to their word, unless pressed to do so. And thus, given that knowledge, and by the King's orders, we had already chopped a large enough hole in the back wall of the city to lead the horses through, by the time the first wave of hail fire fell. And what did not burn on its own accord, we lit with fire, and escaped westward, concealed within the black thick shield of smoke and ash, and by a lingering dense blanket of fog."

Timothy spoke out from his place in the rear of the line. "What I don't understand though is, how did you know to come save us? Seems kind of lucky, don't you think?"

"Oh, yes. I've skipped that part, didn't I?" Asa said, taking a bit of cooked dragon meat from his pouch, for it was nearly lunch time by then. "It was decided, that I, as the most seasoned huntsman in the regiment, would follow the Queen's captors at a safe distance, and would report her whereabouts afterward, if I could not easily secure her myself... Which led me then, on a back route up the mountain, and I'd nearly overtaken them, when I heard the far off cries of a lady in dire distress, and so I came as swiftly as I could... and the rest you know," he ended with.

"Huh, is that right?" Timothy said, mostly to himself, and grinning slightly.

"What is it now?" Barbara asked, not entirely liking Timothy's now familiar boyish grin.

"Oh, it's nothing," he answered back. "I was just thinking how we'd both have been roasted alive and eaten by a dragon, if you hadn't been such a foul jumper," he smirked slyly.

"Oh, shut it, will you?" she said, and pounded him, good and hard in the arm.

Not particularly ladylike of her, to say the least, but she was very sure he'd had it coming.

In the relative shelter of an open cave, by the warmth of a meager coal fire, Asa sat up with them late after nightfall, recounting the histories of Gleomu, but only so far as their written histories would account for, which in their case only allowed for roughly eight centuries of known history. These were the stories of a dynasty of kings, and great battles against distant waring nations, and the construction and fortification of

117

Ismere. And all the while, Barbara seemed to delight in Asa's every word, like there was no other thing more interesting she'd have liked to hear about.

But Timothy, however, who'd had a natural inclination to history, especially military histories, he began to get a foul taste in his mouth, and grew sick to his stomach, so that he could not stand to even listen, after a short while. His forehead began to pool beaded drops of sweat. And Asa was the first to diagnosis it; He was ill, and what a sorry place for it.

"Was it the dragon meat?" Barbara asked, while folding a wet cloth over his brow.

And to that, Asa replied, that it was possible, but unlikely that that had anything to do with it. (Howbeit, if I might interject my thoughts about the matter, I would say that given Timothy's eating habits, while his grandmother was away: How he ate almost nothing but whole custards and tart pastries, and drank only milk, it's a wonder he had not become violently ill much sooner.)

That being said, it was a bitter cold night for Timothy, in the cave, even with Asa's extra bedroll blanketed across his shoulders.

When the sun arose, it was suggested that Timothy should be left in the cave with supplies, enough for his remaining time in Gleomu, and that Barbara and Asa would go on without him.

However, Barbara, as a mark to her kindness, said she couldn't stand to leave him alone, not with dragons and giants, or whatever other foul thing might find him. Likewise, Timothy also would not bear to be left out of the mission. And so, because of their protests, they went along the now rockier trail, at a quarter pace, giving Timothy plenty of opportunity for rest, and more than his fair share of water rations.

And although it may be crude to mention, Timothy, who'd for a long time prided himself on his digestional integrity, and an iron clad constitution, did begin to vomit around midday. And, as a result, has ever since been unable to stomach even moderate portions of dragon meat (which is especially good in soups, if you care for such a thing).

His thigh muscles and knees ached, his joints felt both stiff and warm, if that could be possible, but at last they came to an opening in the trail, as a wet snow began to fall in full flakes onto their faces.

"Finally," Timothy said hoarsely, throwing his arms wide and letting the largest flakes melt against his boiling forehead. But he soon began to cough, deeply and grossly, and found it hard to stop.

Their path widened considerably, and as they crested over the top of a small hill they noticed they'd come into what seemed to be a shallow valley, with low walls surrounding it, like the crater of a moon. They continued on for what felt like an eternity. Until the sun had faded into dusk, and the pale condensed moonlight hit upon a very peculiar sight indeed.

These first grainy beams struck upon a house, only a stone throw's distance away from them, the light reflecting off it like a mirror, or a pool of water. And then the full structure came into view, as if it had appeared as a ripple out of thin air.

"Dear me," Barbara gasped. "Any darker and we would have passed by this house entirely."

And then Asa spoke up, as they all stopped to take in the sight of such an elaborate, two-storied stone house, strangely positioned in the center of miles and miles of ravenous sinister mountains.

"I'm not so sure of that," he said.

"What do you mean?" Barbara asked.

"As I see it, we've been walking along in this odd valley since before sunset, and how is it that we've only just now seen this strange building?" Asa explained.

"You mean like... an invisible house?" Timothy said frailly.

"Just the sort, dear prince," he replied. And then to himself, " ...Or a house that can be invisible when it wishes."

And then Asa spoke these words, which made apparent what should have been plainly obvious this entire time.

"What curious place is this?" he said, as they kept their gazes upon that now visible house, with its meticulously trimmed lawn behind a rod iron gate, and the familiar welcoming glow of lamp light in the upper glass-paned windows, and the tasteful stone moldings and cornices near the entryway.

And it was at just that moment that Timothy, even as sickly as he was, and Barbara both, had realized a simple truth. To them, this was not a curious place, to them it was exactly what they might expect from any respectable english estate. And to them, both coming from wealthier parentage, it was something that they had seen so often that they'd hardly taken notice of it anymore. But to Asa, who was not an Englishman, to him this was an entirely peculiar residence, unlike any he'd ever seen.

This was a house of Earth. And with that realization, Timothy's head began to swim, and his eyes blurred their focus. The exhaustions of the day, and of the previous night, had finally overtaken him. And the last thing he could hear, echoing and fading into a thick darkness, was Barbara's expression of shock.

"Oh!" she gasped, trying to reach for his head before it hit the hard sanded ground.

Darkness.

CHAPTER TWENTY-FIVE

AWAKEN

✦

His eyes squinted. Little fingers of warm sunlight peeked through the dense blood-red and gold woven curtains. A moderate flame burned in the fireplace, and a cold rag was rolled upon his forehead.

He was wrapped up snuggly in an embroidered feather blanket, but startling and most disturbingly, was an unfamiliar old man and a metal spoon in his face. The old man spoke, and the words mushed inside Timothy's memory, "Eat this. You must eat. You'll feel better, I assure you."

But these words drifted and quieted in his mind and were lost in the place of dreams. And darkness, once more.

In the morning, he awoke to a spectacularly wonderful and properly made up bedroom quarters. His pillows sunk in like clouds, and he was both comfortable, and noticeably and gratefully warm. But that was soon hard to fully appreciate, being that his stomach began to growl loudly, for he had not eaten.

This unexpected situation was both familiar and unnatural, pleasant and yet strangely unsettling.

"Where is everyone?" he thought to himself, as he slid into a pair of fur lined slippers that were set out for him.

And he began to rehearse in his head the events that had led him to this point: First Hrim, and the cliff, and then the dragon, and Asa, and the invisible english home.

Upon examination of the room, he found that both his satchel and his sword had gone missing, and he felt at first ashamed for letting them out of his sight, but had soon realized that that had been unavoidable.

And so, given his newly unfortunate situation, he did what he thought to be the only reasonable course of action. Stoking an iron fire poker into the hottest coals in his fireplace he waited, and still famished and utterly weak from having been so sick, he crept out that beautifully carved door, and down the elegantly carpeted hallway, his footsteps hushly silenced inside furry house shoes. Paintings from all corners of antiquity hung upon the walls as he lightly stepped down the wide illustrious staircase, with a high stained-glass window, and with a blazing hot fire poker held up and ready to strike at any fiend who might dare attack him.

Which given the present setting does sound silly, but you must remember that they had not so long ago been tracking the horse prints of an obvious enemy, who had watched with displaced apathy the burning of Hrim, assuming every soul in that city had perished in a restless, unquenchable fire, and who had taken his grandmother away, captive, and this might very well have been that enemy's hideout. And, to be true, an enemy's lair is an enemy's lair, no matter how comfortable or fancy it might appear.

Once down the stairs, he heard a rattling sound ricocheting off the marble floors and high coffered ceiling, and not a loud sound but a discernible and casual noise; Timothy heard pleasant conversation. And then, strangely a voice he'd thought to never hear again, with a chuckling wobble in the way that he spoke, as if he were always laughing, or never without a joke.

"Oh, oh... and tell them, Darius, if you will, about how you've got here. It's such a remarkable story, and I know I've grown rather found of hearing it," said the voice of his grandfather, Wilbur.

Timothy let his hot iron poker dip to the ground, his defenses had been almost instantly broken with shock. His grandfather, whom he'd thought to have been dead for nearly a year, was now alive, really alive. Stepping forward, as if drawn uncontrollably, he came quickly into a festive and lavishly prepared dining hall, in which three sizable tables were pressed together to form a "U" shape, and covered over with goblets and silver serving trays, grapes and hams, hard-boiled eggs, and juices and porridge oats. And there at the tables were Barbara, and Matilde, and his grandfather, Wilbur. All seated around, and presenting their full attention to a slender and stately old man, who was most obviously their host, and who had been just about to begin a story, before Timothy had barged in to break the mood.

"Oh. You're awake," the old man said, as if a blink of unsettledness had just blown through his mind, but *that* he had quickly brushed aside.

"Good morning, Tim," Barbara almost shouted, welcoming him to have a seat, at that bountiful table, next to hers.

This was perhaps the most pleasant Barbara had ever been to him, and so Timothy could not help but to stare, pondering for a brief second at why she had been so uncharacteristically cordial. And in so doing this, Timothy set his now much less heated fire poker down on the marble floor by his new chair.

"Where are we?" Timothy asked, pulling up to the table.

"Well, at my house, of course," said the old man, as if that had answered it.

"Yes, yes, Timothy," his grandfather spoke up, while cutting through a slice of baked ham. And looking down at his plate first, he said, "This man here, is Darius D'Moncure, as good a scientist and an Englishmen as you would hope to meet." His grandfather finished, chuckling peculiarly.

Timothy scratched on his chin, and through his hair, trying to get his brain around this thought.

"So... you're not a prisoner, here?" he asked.

But his grandfather did not answer right away, though he hardly could have, because of the way that Darius had interjected himself, leaning forward and placing his hands on top of the center table, for he had been standing.

"No, no. Don't be silly... have you ever *heard* of such a thing?" Which caused such a strange laugh to go up from the group.

And Matilde, who was seated across from he and Barbara at the other table, in a seat pushed up closely to Wilbur's, she said very convincingly, "Ha! No, child. We're his guests."

And although this had seemed to be the most ideal turn of events, it had also felt strangely eerie. Which is possibly why Timothy began to ask this next question.

"How long was I asleep?" he turned to ask Barbara, who looked blank faced, as if she were trying to remember something told to her.

"Since..." she began to say, drawing out her words.

"Since yesterday," Darius interrupted, helping her along.

"Oh yes, that's right. Since yesterday," she answered more confidently. "We've just arrived last night."

And that is when Timothy remembered something, so vitally important. "No," he said scratching his head, and then pointing at the old man. " ...but weren't you in my room yesterday?" he asked.

For a flash of a second the old man's eyes appeared to shift, as if taken by surprise, but then he smiled reassuringly. "Oh no, of course not, that was this morning."

"Oh, I see," Timothy answered, feeling himself becoming more docile, as if the smell of that great meal presented before him was all that he could clearly think of.

"Are you hungry?" the old man grinned.

"Ye- Yes, very much," Timothy answered, fumbling over his words at first.

And like he hadn't barely a choice in the matter, and because he was in actuality so feverishly hungry, Timothy nodded blankly that he would begin to eat, and Barbara helped him with a plate full of turkey, and sliced baked apples with cinnamon and crumbled breading, chocolate whipped puddling, and creamy danishes; And more food than would be natural for anyone to eat in a normal breakfast.

A golden spoonful of baked apples, and the world and his mind grew foggier.

And as he licked the sugared syrup off the spoon of his first bite, he turned to ask Barbara a very serious question, and one that should not have been overlooked.

"Where's Asa?" he asked.

"Who?" she asked in return, as if she had not understood his question.

CHAPTER TWENTY-SIX

THE HOUSE

W hat a perfectly splendid home, in every way. After only a few hours, Timothy was fairly certain that he'd never had so much fun in all his life, nor had he ever wanted for anything less, than when he was there, a visitor in Darius's spectacular estate.

His was a house of invention and science, and on that account Timothy's grandfather had not exaggerated, when he called their host, "as good a scientist... as you would ever hope to meet."

A lawn, made specifically to be always green and trimmed, without water. Beds that would tuck themselves in, and a kitchen that could make food through compounds and formulas, and chemical equations and appropriate temperatures, so that anything you wished to eat could be made for you, as quickly as a modern-day microwave oven, yet even sweeter and more appetizing than regular foods. These were the exact ideal variations of every dish and delicacy, the bests of every food, in their juiciest and most gratifying state. A house where all things were given freely and nothing was required, no work nor labor for anything, nor lack of comfort at anytime.

And the whole building, in all its glories, was run entirely by the light from the sun, which was Darius's particular field of interest. For truly, though he was no amateur in all the areas of science, and indeed a master at most, he would more rather describe himself as a luminologist.[ãä]

And every mealtime was a wonder to behold, and Darius told the most magnificent stories. For as it would appear, in our world, this man had dedicated a prominent portion of his life to the study and collection of artifacts and antiquities. (That is to say, things of the past that were at one time brilliant and revolutionary, but have long since faded from our memories, to be forgotten.)

"And when I retired," he told them, around a dinner of crepes, and caviar, and radish salad with sweet dressing. "I'd decided to make a home for myself, here, where I would have plenty of freedom to imagine the world as it should be."

Barbara's eyes filled with concern.

"But don't you ever get lonely?" she asked.

"Of course not," Darius said, holding up a glass of dark red wine, as if to toast to them. "I have my guests."

With those words, Wilbur and Matilde, and Barbara and Timothy, all lifted their cups in return to cheer and applaud him, for who could imagine then, a world more wonderful than Darius had made for them.

ãä Or a studier of light and all it pertains to, especially focusing on the luminescence of living organisms.

"See you in the morning," Timothy said, as he headed down the hall to his bedroom.

"Goodnight," Barbara replied, and went to reach for the handle of her door.

"See you in the morning," Timothy repeated, his feet sinking further into the deep hall carpet.

"Goodnight," Barbara answered, and went to reach for her door handle.

"Wait," Timothy interrupted, halting and unnerving her. Barbara stopped midway, with her hand still gripping the half-turned doorknob.

"Didn't we just do this?" he asked, seeming frightfully confused.

"Ah... no, I don't think so," she answered.

"You're acting strange, Tim. Is something wrong?" And the way that she phrased this, was as you would if you'd thought someone were slowly going mad, but wanted to spare their feelings.

"Ye- Yes... of course there is," he scratched his head, and answered, as if he were trying to remember something, something lost, something vitally important.

And this was his reply, "See, I just said, 'See you in the morning'," he began to explain, as he came back to stand with her at her door, and he spoke softly so that no one would overhear, though he was not exactly sure why that mattered.

"And you answered, 'Goodnight', and then we did it again, almost exactly the same as before."

Barbara's look was still questioning.

"Don't you remember?" Timothy asked again.

She said, seeming like she wished to help him, "No, sorry, I don't."

And then she did a very natural, yet however mothering, thing to do.

"Are you ill?" she asked, and put the back of her hand to his forehead. "No, you don't feel heated."

"Of course I'm not ill," Timothy retorted. "Would you just listen..." And then like a flash upon his brain, he began to remember.

"No... but I was, I was sick, when we got here."

"Oh, yes," Barbara's eyes began to blink as if she were awakening. "I'd forgotten all about that."

"We had to carry you to bed, you'd fainted-"

"We? Who's we?" Timothy interrupted.

And Barbra closed her eyes tightly, tilting her head upward, as if trying to wrench the memories back into her consciousness.

"It was me... and," she stammered. "Me and-"

Her eyes shot open, she had just remembered it all. They both had.

"Asa," they said together.

Their expressions now instantly grave and serious, reminiscent of wild animals caught in a poacher's trap, and knowing for the first time the sense of real danger, imminent danger: The kind you must either escape from, or be lost to forever.

CHAPTER TWENTY-SEVEN

MAKING AMENDS

✦

L ate after midnight, tip-toeing in a delicate silence, in pairs of borrowed soft-soled house slippers, Timothy and Barbara tried to make amends for a many number of extraordinary dinners and scrumptious breakfasts, when all the while their traveling companion and guide had been caught up in a very real and obvious peril, if he was even still alive.

However, it was quite a troubling thing to go poking through a potentially murderous trap of a house, when you have no idea where exactly to begin, nor any clear idea as to where your enemy might be lurking, in shadows or crevice, or behind every closed doorway. So they began, slowly moving outward from their rooms, holding their breath, cautiously creaking open heavy doors to check for any sign of Asa, or any clues about his fate, still unknown.

The first door in the creepily decorated upstairs hall. Nothing. An old squatty study with books on every wall, nothing else.

They dared not separate: Firstly, that would be too dangerous, and although it might make for quieter and less detectible searching, they could not risk the chance of being caught alone. And secondly, they felt, at that time, they had needed both of their combined willpowers, so not to fall back into that mindless, relentless trance again. And deeply, although they pushed it aside, were the longing pangs calling them back into a world where everything was safely comfortable and pleasant for them; But this was not the real world. That fake world was a prison, as much as any barred cage or shackle, and they did better to remember that together. And it helped to speak the words in a whisper.

"Don't go back. Don't go back," Timothy said, under his breath, as they searched the upstairs rooms. Until the danger of that prison became more real to him, little by little.

As it moved from something they desired, to something they disliked, to something they might eventually learn to loath. Yet, for now, they felt its draw.

Empty. Every room in the upstairs hall was empty.

And, if one might care about this sort of thing given the situation, all of those rooms were cleverly decorated in a tasteful early 1900's fashion, but in none of them were Asa, Timothy's grandparents, nor their captor, Darius. And in all of them, thoughtfully removed was anything that might have remotely been used as a weapon; Obviously decorative swords had been taken off the walls, and likewise candles were set onto saucers instead of atop candlestick holders, and, of course, every fire poker was removed.

And when finally the last room had been searched through, Timothy started to moan, frustrated with himself for having lost his sword. But Barbara graciously reassured him, that he ought not be so hard on himself, even admitting that she had not only lost her own dagger, but Asa as well, and in the end, she suggested that if they were forced now to go into the main portions of the house, that night, without weapons, then it would be best to use disguises.

"Like how?" Timothy asked. "What sorts of things did you have in mind?"

"Oh, you know," she answered. "We could dress in our nightclothes, wrap up in blankets, and pretend to be headed to the kitchen for a midnight snack."

"That's genius, Cholley," Timothy congratulated her. But as he was considering the prospect his eyes grew wide and unsettled. "Oh, no..." he said.

"What is it?" Barbara asked.

"Who's ever heard of *two people* headed down to the kitchen for a midnight snack?" he exclaimed, in whispered tones. "We have to separate, or our disguises are no good."

"Oh, bother..." Barbara sighed. "Do you think we can hold off the trance without each other?"

"We've no choice," Timothy answered, and they both knew he was right.

CHAPTER TWENTY-EIGHT

DOWNSTAIRS

The stairs beneath Timothy's feet were fashioned of polished stones and were carpeted, so that they did not squeak. However, this was of little comfort to him.

It was blindingly dark that night. The moon was only a sliver in the sky, and its ineffective rays shone in dark colors through the stained glass window above the stairway. As he got to the first landing, Timothy looked behind him to see the faint silhouette of his companion at the top of the staircase, just a black figure with long hair against an even darker background.

Holding the railing to keep his balance, the stone felt cold in his hands, and so he was glad, if only for a disguise, that he had brought a fuzzy fleece blanket to wrap up warmly in.

His first step finally hit the bottom of the staircase. He made sure not to scuff his feet along the marble floor, lifting each step gently.

Through an open doorway, the dining room appeared lifeless and empty, though quite possibly the faint aromas of baked pies and cakes, and cooked glazed ham still lingered in the air. A pulling sensation in his chest, Timothy felt the urge inside of him to have just one last look. It was dark, and who would know. He wouldn't have to taste the food, only to be around it might be enough, he thought. Perhaps, there were leftovers from this evening in the kitchen.

He took a half-step forward and then another, without any effort at all. Clouded fogginess began to seep into his mind again.

"*No!*" his thoughts yelled inside his brain.

With all his strength, he pressed his hands up against the doorposts, to keep himself out of the dining room.

"*Asa, Asa...*" he repeated. And mumbled, now audibly, "Don't go back. Don't go back," he said in repetition, and willfully pulling himself away from the dining room, and from that beastly kitchen, he took steps away from there, until the smell became less noticeable, and less appealing.

Several open parlors, and sitting areas, but nothing of significance. The first door he opened downstairs was a broom closet, then an empty bedroom, and then a laboratory study with beakers, and filled up chalkboards, and a sturdy leather book laid closed upon the desk.

And then another bedroom, except this one occupied by his grandparents (and he knew this, because of Wilbur's telltale snore coming from the far side of the bed).

As if by reflex, Timothy thought to wake them, until he realized that they had not yet been shaken from their trances, and that it would be too loud at the present time to try to convince them of it. And so reluctantly he shut the door, wishing he could do more.

"*Asa, first,*" he thought, and afterward he had planned to come back for them.

Another door, a heavy double door, stretching across the entire width at the end of the hallway; This one carved with fanciful markings, that in the nighttime cast troubling dark shadows on its face. No question about it, this was Darius's quarters, he thought. And that understood, looking over its sinister state, he made up his mind, to enter there only in the case that he'd exhausted all other options.

Rustling behind the door, their enemy was awake. Timothy ran, trying to let his footsteps fall softly on the hard marble slabs. And just as he was out of sight, around the corner, the door unlatched with an echo, and Darius emerged, bearing an electric light in one hand, and a thick metallic walking cane, with a duck head handle, that sharply clanked on the floor with each new step, like a blacksmith's mallet.

Fortunately, Timothy tucked inside an open parlor as the first rays of Darius's electric candle illuminated the hall. And from his new hiding place behind an elegant sofa, he saw his enemy come and halt in front of the broom closet door, the same door he'd unsuccessfully searched just moments earlier. And with the press of a secret button on the side of his cane, Darius waved it across the closet door. Something had activated, and Timothy could hear the sound of rock sliding against rock.

The door opened, shining light onto a set of new stairs, like castle stairs, winding lower into a basement or dungeon, or whatever should be hidden beneath them.

Not giving time to think of how dangerous this might be, though realizing this might be his only chance at it, Timothy left his hiding place, creeping up quickly behind Darius, his footsteps almost inaudible, silent in his cushy house slippers, just as the back of the broom closet wall closed behind him. He would have rejoiced, except for this new haunting sense that he was now, even more so, hopelessly trapped, as rays from Darius's electric light shone upward, reflecting in a low glow off the walls of the winding staircase.

Leaving the only thing to be done: to follow that light, but not too closely, and to pray, against very foul odds, that he would not be caught.

CHAPTER TWENTY-NINE

FINDING THINGS

I n the meanwhile, you might wonder what Barbara had done, left alone in the upstairs of that creepy house, wrapped up tightly in her blanket, and house slippers, and nightclothes. She paced back and forth, between her room and the top of the stairs. All the while, imagining what deadly horror Timothy was getting himself into.

Until she could no longer wait the full twenty or so minutes, which was the time when they'd agreed she should follow after, if Timothy had not yet returned. (And this was of course an approximate measure of time, for in that house they had no clock or watch. Yet, notwithstanding, even without a timepiece Barbara realized she was being premature.) Howbeit, she could not rest even a second longer, as she balanced her feet down the monstrously darkened staircase.

And just as she had reached the first landing she heard the sound of scraping stone, and saw Darius entering a hidden cellar passageway, and Timothy ducking in after him. She tried to wave him off, motioning for him to stop, but the passage closed and she was abandoned, left completely alone.

Barbara ran past the dining hall, and in vain, she scoured through the closet, and on the outside wall, for anything that might be a switch or a hidden lever, but nothing.

This was not that sort of secret passage. Darius himself had taken its only key, his cane, inside, down through the stairwell underneath the house, and the door was locked impenetrably behind him.

Barbara kicked the wall, and let a small tear roll down her face, thinking of what might happen to Timothy. Until she gained her composure, coming to realize a very helpful fact. She was left alone, and with that knowledge she knew she could now snoop uninhibited through the main halls, for at least the next few minutes, without fear of being caught.

With this in mind, she soared through the main floor, examining each room as thoroughly and as rapidly as she could. Running through parlors and sitting rooms, until she came to a laboratory study, with its vials and beakers of odd colored mixtures, and its chalkboards, filled in every corner with mathematical formulas, and strange diagrams.

Lighting the half portion of a candle she found, a glow of burning light expanded through the room, illuminating the chalkboards. On the smaller boards, there were mostly numbers and figures, though on one she spotted a sketch of some intricate flying contraption.

But when the light from her candle fell upon the main chalkboard, it showed a massive and detailed scientific schematic for some great machine, with what looked like a huge cupped wind vane at the top, and then bundles of wires leading to strange capacitors. It was precise, and Barbara thought, sinister, although she could not tell exactly how or why she knew this, she just felt it, down to the pit of her stomach.

"The time," she thought.

Perhaps she'd been searching for too long, and speedily she went to extinguish the candle, to place it back on the desk where she'd found it, but that's when she noticed it. A book, hefty and leather bound, as big as a church bible, it lay shut upon the desk.

And being herself naturally curious, and thinking she could spare just a few more minutes, she opened to the last written page, and began to read.

Tracing the path of the dim light, winding down further and further beneath the house, Timothy followed down the staircase, trying to place his feet in sync with the echo of footsteps, so to remain unheard. Except that he lost his balance in the overlapping shadows, and almost silently, he scuffed his shoes against the edge of a stair.

The footsteps below him and the traveling light stopped. He stopped. Breaths with no noise, nor subtlest sound, escaped his mouth and lungs. The footsteps below him and the light continued. He continued.

Barbara, dragging her finger across the thick coarse paper, to gather in every word by low candle light, this is what she read:

Day 26,283 – Recent frequency measurements indicate a viable light transfer tomorrow morning, will prep the test subject for an eight o'clock transport.

And in like manner, the whole book was filled with similar entries, as one might keep a journal, only this one was scribbled full of study findings and vague scientific discoveries.

Reviewing older entries Barbara found the date when she and Timothy had arrived, and she was happy to learn that she had only lost two days of her memories. Which was hard enough to take as it is, and she could not even imagine what it must be like for Timothy's grandfather, who'd lost nearly a full year of his life by then.

Day 26,281 – The boy is still feverish and ill, and could not eat this morning. He and the girl, however, do have substantial traces of a carrier signal inside of them, of a similar nature as the woman's, and so it can be deduced that they've originated from the same source. Vis-à-vis, if the initial transfer test should prove unsuccessful, then they will both serve as proper alternates.

The native has shown himself to be strikingly

resistant, and uncooperative, but I hold out that he might still make for a worthy assassin, given adequate conditioning.

The stairs opened into a colossal room with a high domed ceiling, all thick stone, and in the center, this towering machine that in the twilight of that cavernous room looked to be roughly the shape and size of a great tree, with bundles of wire and piping leading up to a slowly spinning, massive turbine at the top, like four long cupped branches; And this turning made a deep and steady hum, and every so often, electric sparks would jump up the wired trunk of the machine, leaping from one apparatus to another.

Plainly, the entire room was dedicated to this ghastly mechanism, and Timothy was quite sure that someone as maniacal as their captor, Darius, would not have spent the years and years it must have taken to build such a device unless it was something very powerful, and set to be used for ill intended purposes.

Candlelight flickered in shadows across the pages, as Barbara thumbed through the weighty scientific diary.

Every now and then, coming upon accounts of orb light being recorded in the southern night sky, but the vast part of it was beyond her knowledge of science, and so giving up on any real understanding, she flipped quickly to the first page.

Day 1 –

I am marooned.

Arthur[iv] will pay for this, for his crimes against me, against human accomplishment. Such an illogical half-wit. Can't he see how foolish he is to keep our discoveries hidden from the world? I should have murdered him when I had the chance.

I will avenge myself, and return to Earth somehow. I will be avenged.

From that mammoth center room, there spread out in a jagged circle, many small hallways and passages: like light beams traveling away from the sun, or like the tentacles of an octopus. And out from one of those halls, there burned a constant, weak distant light, melded with flashes of an intense striking light that made crackling noises, and they were always followed by the painful cries of a man, of a familiar voice.

"*Asa,*" Timothy thought.

And sneaking in closer toward the light, he saw that

<hr />

[iv] *Arthur Greyford*

he was indeed right, howbeit he wished he hadn't been.

In a small barred cage, heavy black metal bars, sat Asa, hunched and huddled in the center, he looked exhausted, tormented and very weak.

"Sir, you do not seem to understand your status," Darius proclaimed, standing outside the cage, speaking down to Asa, as if he were not even human.

"All that is required, a simple 'yes', nothing more..." he spoke tenderly now, but even Timothy as far away as he was could sense the true viciousness behind his words.

"If you are silent, there will be repercussions. If you say 'no', there will be consequences," he said now more angrily, but was instantly switched again to false tenderness. "But a 'yes'... and all this pain and consequence will be removed. Don't you want that?" Darius asked.

But Asa, taking all his strength to sit upon his knees, his face was harsh and ragged, he began to laugh, forcefully.

"You call this pain?" he uttered.

Yet as quickly as the words had left his mouth, a shock, like lightning from the end of Darius's cane, as he shoved it into Asa's side, and there again Timothy heard the awful sounds of pain. And seeing him in such a state, made all the baked sugared apples, and candied treats that Timothy had gorged himself on since they'd arrived, it made the memory of them taste noticeably sour in his mouth.

But his laughing only maddened Darius all the more, who said that he would actually prefer it if Asa would starve. And without another word, Darius's echoing footsteps and electric light turned and went straight toward Timothy. And Timothy, retreating from the light, found a secure place in another hallway to hide in, until Darius's steps could be heard up the winding stairs.

And after some more minutes, when all was silent, and he thought he'd waited long enough to be safe, Timothy went slowly, using the pale bursts of electric spark light from that towering machine to find his way. And there in the heavy metal cage, locked up like an animal, he found Asa.

"I'm sorry I took so long," Timothy said, crouching by the cage door, in the nearly pitch black hallway, but with those words a very horrible and dangerous thing happened.

Immediately, the hallway lit up with a blindingly stark, electric glaring beam, and there was Darius, standing just over Timothy showing an evil expression.

"I knew you were there," he sneered.

A burst of electric lightning into his back. Pain beyond our imagining, his muscles seized up, and Timothy lay unconscious on the cold dungeon floor.

"*The time*," Barbara thought again, and knew she had stayed longer than was safe to do so.

Puffing out the candle, she half ran in her fuzzy slippers, nightdress, and blanket around her shoulders, down the hall, and bounding up the stairs, returning to her own door, just as the sound of stone against stone was heard from the downstairs closet passageway.

Barbara delicately twisted the handle, and slid well beneath her covers, hoping she would not be found out. Meanwhile, Darius, taking his deadly cane in hand, marched heavily and loudly down the main hall, clinking his cane on the ground, so that Barbara heard it even with her door shut, and while folded well below her bedcovers.

The noise stopped, and Darius, seeing his laboratory door had been left open a small crack, went to investigate, and found his ledger closed upon the desk, just as it had been, but the table candle melted slightly lower than he'd remembered, and with a fresh pool of wax ringed around the candle base.

A few moments later, Barbara heard her bedroom door creak open, and saw an electric lamp partially illuminating even the space beneath her bedsheets with cracks of discomforting light.

"Up so late, dear heart?" came an old man's voice from the open doorway.

Her insides sank, as a breath of shock entered through her nostrils.

CHAPTER THIRTY
THE MACHINE

✦

F luttering his eyes in the darkness, Timothy awoke with his mind aching, and head lain stiffly on the cold stone floor. By the flashes of intervalic spark light, he could tell he was in the great room of the dungeon, locked into his own separate cage. And among other things, he noticed immediately the burning sensation in all his muscles, like he'd run for days without water.

"Timothy, you're alive!" Barbara exclaimed. And there his eyes focused on another cage far to his right.

"Barely," he moaned, willing his hands to lift himself off the floor, and then leaning his back against the metal cage bars.

For a moment, there was a hopeless sort of pause.

"He's going to torture us, until we eat again, you know," Timothy eventually broke the silence.

"Sorry, but it's worse than that," she said, loud enough to be heard clearly across the wide room.

"What do you mean by that?" he asked.

Though, if Timothy had been close enough he would have seen the disturbed expression on her face as she said this. "He's going to experiment on us," she said. "I know all about it. I read through his journal."

"You did?" Timothy said, eyebrows raised, with a tone of unbelief. "What else did it say?"

"It said, he was going to try some awful thing on your grandmother, first, and if that didn't work, then he'd use us as alternates."

"If it didn't work..." Timothy reiterated. "Like if he killed her?"

"Maybe," Barbara answered, but sounding like she'd mostly agreed with Timothy's reasoning. "He said, it had something to do with frequencies, and a light transfer... which I think means-"

But Timothy interrupted, "That he means to steal our only way home," still painfully resting against the metal bars.

"Exactly," Barbara answered, almost too preoccupied now by their present state, to worry all that much that Timothy had just stolen her prime chance to sound logical and smart.

Frustrated, that he had been caught, and that they seemed to be inexhaustibly trapped, Timothy hit his head against the wall of his barred cage. And then another sound, of grinding stone, and malicious footsteps down the long winding stairs.

The steps as they descended grew more inescapable, and after a minute, two figures settled into the room: Matilde Wolcott, the Queen of Earth, being directed about like a barnyard animal, with forceful nudges from a black metal cane, and Darius, following behind and holding up a stark glaring light, and prodding her onward.

Matilde's face was blank and expressionless, her mind obviously still confined within a heavy trance. Darius led her to a pedestal near the base of that giant tree-like mechanism, locking her forearms and ankles into golden metal straps. And the windmilled turbine atop the machine began to spin more quickly, as if power were being transmitted from Matilde Wolcott to the machine, like she were some human battery source, or an engine of some sort. The tree machine's hummings swelled to a higher pitch. Its sparks shot out more frequently and violently, climbing up the wires on its trunk-like portion.

And even in her comatose state, Mrs. Wolcott's face now showed signs of wincing pain.

"You're hurting her. Stop it!" Barbara yelled out from her cage, which was closest to Darius, and Timothy's closest to his grandmother.

And he, their captor, twisting knobs and flipping switches, and pressing buttons on some ornate control panel, turned to give her some attention.

"Child, I'll do as I like," he said, and reaching inside his coat pocket he retrieved a yellowish-red medium-sized piece of fruit, tossing it into Barbara's cage.

"Here, have an apple," he said snidely. "You'll feel better, I assure you."

"You monster," Barbara shot back, hurling her apple back at Darius, so that he'd had to duck his head.

"Tut, tut," he said as a warning, and flashing a small spark out of his cane to show her his seriousness.

And returning again to the controls, he spoke over his shoulder, "You are not informed enough to make such a claim." And throwing the final switch, he said, "Let history decide who I am, and who I am not." His words arrogant and face greedily proud.

The machine roared in high-pitched swirling madness, massive sparks leapt along the wires. Timothy's grandmother cried out in searing agony. Whatever Darius's dastardly monstrous machine was doing, it could only be for the worse.

Timothy could not bear to see his grandmother this way, and so he shut his eyes tightly. And in the corner of his mind, separate from the chaos in the room, was another ringing, a distinct tone that he had heard once before. A ringing that grew more loudly in his ears, drowning away everything else. Light began to expand outward filling his cage, in the shape of a glowing emanating sphere of light. The room outside the orb was now completely silenced. Timothy saw Darius throw up his hands in rage and yell something, but he could not hear the words.

Unbelievable force, shot so lightning fast toward the ceiling that Timothy rocketed between the spinning cupped blades and through the stone, and through the ground above: Out of that world entirely, as instant as a camera's flash bulb.

CHAPTER THIRTY-ONE

EARTH

When Timothy landed back in Mayfield, in the window room, he found that hidden gable room enclosed within an ever widening sphere of electrified gold-colored energy. It was much like the orb by which he had just traveled, only many times greater, yet seemingly less stable.

Timothy gazed up at the giant sphere surrounding the window room and everything within it, and that's when he realized its true purpose.

"He's not just stealing our *way* home," he said aloud. "He's stealing all of it."

Trapped, Timothy turned all around the room trying to think of something that might stop him, but what? To his knowledge it seemed impossible now to alter this chain of events, to keep Darius from taking the globe and the painting, and the entire room. But maybe, he thought, he might have just enough time to use them once more, before they were gone forever.

Wooden beams breaking like twigs, the walls being shattered away from the rest of the house. The entire window room, with most of its walls and ceiling, was being wrenched into the air above the nighttime English countryside.

Timothy could barely get to the almanac[3], as the room rattled and shook through the air, like it were being pulled upward through an earthquake. He snatched up the heavy book, almost toppling over as he tumbled toward the globe, and holding the immense old book, cupped in the cradle of his left arm, he shouted the numbers aloud as he fumbled to set the dials and switches.

And with the last switch thrown, the painting came alive again, showing the images and topography of Gleomu like a glowing atlas. He spun the crank vigorously to charge its internal mechanisms. The shaking became more and more violent; items fell from the desk and an elegant Grecian statued bust tipped from its pedestal and slid across the wood planked floor.

Light spun outward in colored circles from the globe, all was ready. Yet, before he could touch the globe's face he was thrown off his feet, as the room and himself were exploded toward the stars with a boom that echoed like a hundred cannons all being fired at once.

From over his shoulder, through the missing portions of wall and floor where the room had broken away from the rest of the house, Timothy saw the lights of the Mayfield school, and the surrounding countryside, beginning to fade away into the distance below (like you might see if you were traveling by rocket ship).

---

3 A book that contains information relevant to a specific date. In this case, the almanac is a large ledger book that holds specific coordinates for many of the most interesting planets in our known universe.

And then another flash of brilliant light, and he saw Barbara arrive, blasting through the center of the painting. He had forgotten her in the hectic chaos. Of course, both he and Barbara had made it a point to set out for their rescue mission separately, so that they would return separately, incase something dreadful had happened to either one of them, so that neither would be trapped in Gleomu permanently.

"Honestly?" Barbara said, seeing Timothy knocked from his feet, and still seated on the wood planked floor.

Behind Barbara, the painting jumbled its images for a brief second, like a television set might do, if it's losing its signal.

"Come on," he answered back, stumbling in the quaking room toward the globe.

He set an unsteady finger roughly to where the capitol city might be. Light shot upward toward the bits of the ceiling that remained, causing an obvious disturbance in the electrified orb surrounding the window room.

Timothy reached out his hand for her to take it.

"Where are we going?" she asked, as the signal in the painting grew less and less distinct, and the countryside below them became lesser dots of light. And off along the night horizon could be seen the greater London city lights, but those too soon faded.

"To Ismere, or to Darius. You take your pick," Timothy said.

"Will we ever come back to Earth?" Barbara asked, seeing London and the blackness of the sea, and all the great cities of Europe through the broken portions of the room. And knowing her parents, on their summer in Madrid, would never have dreamed this would happen to her.

"I don't know," Timothy said, honestly.

And yet, realizing there was no better choice, Barbara took his hand as the light solidified around them.

And from within Darius's giant thieving orb, there was another flash of an even whiter, more radiant light, and the world of Earth was disappeared, in an instant.

CHAPTER THIRTY-TWO

THREATS AND PROMISES

"**O**pen the gates," Timothy shouted to the morning watchman.

The pair now stood at the entrance of the southern gate, after landing quite off the mark, in a nearby recently deserted hamlet of the city, and after shattering the roof ridge off an old barn during their blazingly fast descent. The two had run across the fields and were now standing in front of the city, at the entrance of the South Gate, desperately out of breath, and rather impatient with the watchman's remarks, but understandably so.

"Under whose authority," the watchman answered, knowing that an hour after the warning bells had rung, the city gates were to be barred shut, not to be reopened for any reason, or so were his orders.

"Under... his," Barbara yelled to the watchman, pointing toward Timothy. And her companion peered peculiarly back at her, however he was quick to understand her meaning.

"Is that right?" the watchman responded, almost chuckling. "And who might you be, little man?"

And then, with a measure of regalia Timothy had not yet known he'd possessed, he shouted to the man in an even royal tone, "I am the Prince of Earth."

King Corwan and the rest of the survivors from Hrim had rode into the city late during the final watches of the previous night. And at sunrise, the giant's army could be seen marching along the foot of the Hyrdig mountains, and it was commonly thought that they would be ready to make war before nightfall.

Within a half-hour of their arrival, Timothy and Barbara were ushered into a council room within the palace, and were made to give the account of their adventures before the King and Queen, and all of their army's generals; Including the portion of the story in which Asa had been captured and had rather been tortured, than to eat Darius's food. And it was here that Barbara could no longer bear to look directly at the Queen, and to see her face, knowing that she now felt all the more responsible for leaving him (Asa, the Queen's son), and for losing all memory of him as she had.

And finally, when they had come to the end of their stories, Timothy ended with this, "We have six hours left, Your Majesties."

"And then what?" One of the elder generals called out, directing his question mostly at the young prince.

Although, he was not the first to answer. For as everyone there in the council room knew, Queen Delany was by far the most experienced among the sciences of light travel, and so all eyes focused toward her, mostly out of habit.

"It's hard to say, for sure," the Queen answered, somewhat reluctantly. "Even in our younger days, this is unprecedented, unlike anything King Corwan, nor I, have ever seen," And she reached out to take the King's hand, as a comfort for what she was about to say.

"Either you will be reflected back to Earth, to be dropped from heights unknown, where you'd left from," she said, looking empathetically at Timothy, who'd been the last to touch the globe. "Or else, you will follow the window room to wherever Darius takes it."

And then Delany, squeezing more tightly onto Corwan's hand, said something that all there knew better than to oppose.

"But whatever your fate, I will journey with you... Whether to death, or to battle."

Upon those words, all the generals who had not yet been standing, within the overcrowded room, arose from their seats, along with the King (still holding firmly to his wife's hand), all to show their support and honor for their gracious Queen.

In the mid-afternoon, the horde of a thousand giants descended upon the northern gate, many dragging or pulling by rope, or pushing enormous catapults, which were themselves the size of small houses.

These giants, grotesque to look at, with their scarred faces, and missing teeth, or in some cases eyes or noses, they held dangerous spiked wood clubs, or had giant sized hook-tipped swords strapped upon their backs.

Their leader was one named Atilion. He stood nearly a head taller than all other giants, and had only a shallow scar across brow. And when the giant's army had established their ranks, he came to threaten the people of Ismere before the northern gate, defiantly.

Around his waist, a metal skirt of armor like that of an ancient Roman soldier, and a cap style helmet over his broad skull, and an armored plate across his chest, leaving the length of his arms and across his back fully open to attack. The weapon in his hands, a vicious club, like the shape and size of a great oak tree that had been pulled up by the roots, and on the face of the club, cruel long sharpened spikes, each the length of a man's arm. A terrible giant, proud and arrogant, and unmerciful.

"Slaves," Atilion opened wide his arms and said in a low, derisive greeting. "I am your *new* master. Surrender, and you will live under my protection." And the giant bellowed out a ferocious laugh, leaning his weight upon his behemoth club.

With a heavy persuasion, the archers in the towers were forced to hold back their bows, by the King's orders. And Barbara and Timothy saw all this unfold, standing atop the city wall, overlooking the battlements, alongside King Corwan, and Queen Delany, and beside them also many of the royal princes and princesses, who were not busy directing troops elsewhere.

Looking down from the city wall, Timothy knew this was the same giant, with the immeasurable footprints, that had stolen his grandmother away, delivering her to Darius on the cliff's ledge. And deep within his heart, rising up quickly, Timothy felt for the first time a desire to kill a living person, but more for the sake of justice or vengeance, than in cold blood, but still the desire was there and he may have well tried at it, if Atilion had not been a monstrous giant war king. And while Timothy was still contemplating this new anger, he saw King Corwan step to the edge of the city wall to challenge this new foe.

"You are a fool, Atilion," King Corwan pronounced, his royal cape draping down below his waist, and in full armor, holding his helmet at his side. "...A fool, in proportion to your size. You will die today, and your people will pay our kingdom tribute for a hundred years... Or leave, go in peace, and we will not pursue you. Those are our conditions."

"You threaten *me*, little king?" the giant roared in laughter. "We will see who will be threatened."

And Atilion hoisted his club high into the air, giving his signal, calling for the fire boulders that began to rain like hail upon the city, annihilating buildings and marketplaces, and slowly chipping away at the huge quarried stone walls that enclosed the city.

King Corwan and his generals ordered a retaliation attack, launching flaming spears and arrows at the giant's army, but for reason of distance, and by the sheer size of their enemies, its effects were superfluous at best. Only a handful of giants had been slain, and only one of their catapults burned to the ground.

161

Along the wall, soldiers ran from post to post: delivering orders, making adjustments for wind and the giants' movements, and loading towering trebuchets to fling boulders at Atilion's forces. Which did some good, but only against those giants who were not paying attention; For if they were, they could simply move to the side or reposition their catapults and the boulders from Ismere would fall past them, to no effect.

"To the horses," a bearded general cried at the top of his voice. And then there followed the sound of rams horns, calling all cavalryman to the North Gate.

In the courtyard below, Timothy saw King Corwan mounting a grey and white spotted stallion, as the gate chains clanked with the loudest metal clacking, hurrying to be opened.

Unaccustomed to battle, and with no orders of their own, Timothy and Barbara remained where they had been, standing atop the wall, watching the battle unfold, as the fire boulders continued to descend upon the city. And they had just thought to find a proper place for hiding, when they saw the Queen, followed closely by Princess Alethea, rushing up the steps to greet them.

The Queen had just come from bidding long and unshamefully tearful farewells, to her husband and to the five of her sons who would be riding at the head of the attack. (And those sons, in order of age, were: Reuel, the eldest prince, Kalib, who was after Asa in age, then Barak, Hal, and lastly Tahan.)

And in their goodbyes, Princess Alethea had held her father's hand and had jokingly said that he had better kill all these giants before the winter's feast, or else she will not have time enough to prepare her famous lamb's bread; Which, if you'd imagine a meatloaf, is something very similar, only made from lamb's meat.

"Then I had better do my best," Corwan answered her, bending low from his horse to kiss her forehead. And then with calls of war, the cavalrymen, the knights of Ismere, struck out the gate, at a full gallop to meet the giants in battle.

Which I suppose should return us again to Timothy and Barbara, Queen Delany and Princess Alethea at the top of the wall.

In the Queen's hand, she held an extra pair of coarse leather gloves, like the kind a blacksmith might wear, and in the Princess's hands a crossbow and a quiver of arrows she had not had before.

"Here, put these on," the Queen said to Timothy, who was for a moment bewildered by his new gift.

"Gloves, Your Majesty?" he said as a question.

"Yes, and take them," she answered.

And as he was fitting the oversized gloves onto his hands, the Queen began to explain. "As you've said, this Darius fellow has an electrified cane, is that correct?" she continued.

"Yes, Your Majesty," both Timothy and Barbara answered together.

"Very well, then," the Queen replied. "Since leather is a poor conductor of electricity, then we might still be able to use our swords."

And the Queen, Delany, had said "our swords", because Timothy had, since their arrival, been given a new sword to replace the one he'd lost. But, as of yet, Barbara had not received any new weapons.

"And, my dear," were the Queen's words, now directing her attentions to Barbara. "If Ismere should fall, and we will pray that is prevented, but if it does, you will flee with my daughter, Alethea, by the cover of night, across the river Theydor, to Rodor Brook, where you will be safe for the time being, and the Princess will secure your safety."

"Yes, my Queen," Barbara answered with a subtle curtsy, to show that she had understood all the Queen's orders, and because she'd felt it seemed appropriate.

"And for your protection," the Queen continued, motioning toward the Princess to present Barbara with her new crossbow and quiver of arrows, and the stock of the bow was lined with a golden ivy pattern, and the fletching of the arrows looked to be made of bluebird feathers.

"Thank you, Your Majesty," Barbara replied. "They're beautiful," was all she could think to say, for indeed they were.

There were shouts along the wall. In a moment of chaos, a watchman in a nearby tower yelled and rang the town bell to warn of another barrage of catapult fire.

"Artillery!" he screamed, from high in his tower perch.

A new deluge of fire boulders fell throughout the capitol city, and one hit and broke through a part of that seemingly impenetrable city wall, just behind the Queen and Princess Alethea, a part of the wall that had already withstood severe damages.

The royal family, leaping forward to avoid the collapsing wall, the heat from the catapult fire was scorching against their skin. Their walls had been breached; The Queen's expression was of extreme sadness, as if she'd seen a loved one slain before her eyes. (However, that was not it exactly, Queen Delany knew the significance of a wall breach, and that those were the first indications that Ismere had begun to fall to the giant's army. So that a simple break in the wall meant far more than that, such a thing would mean the nearly inevitable deaths of many innocent people.

And if I might add in just one more commentary on the matter: In every region of the kingdom, it was commonly held that Ismere, its flagship city, would never, and for that matter, could never be lost to an enemy's forces, nor be ransacked in battle. Though, this was not the sort of belief that men spoke of openly, as they may talk of weather or political matters. This belief was instilled in their hearts, much like our common belief that the world is round, though most men have never experienced its roundness, firsthand. Yet, even so, it is a founding pillar on which we build our lives.

And much like this, among the citizens of Gleomu, their certainty of Ismere's safety was not something they may have ever consciously believed. They would train in the citizen's army, and work to keep its walls in top repair, but all out of a well developed sense of propriety and good intention, and not out of fear. So that there, on this day, there was a birth of a new fear, and a death of an innocence they had been yet unaware of.)

165

"It's time, Your Majesty," Timothy spoke loudly in the riotousness of the moment.

He could hear the ringing. It was the end of he and Barbara's seven total hours in Ismere, and now he would be reflected away; Either to follow the globe and the window room, to challenge Darius for the safety of those he cared for, or to be dropped from the outer reaches of space, and to see our world below him as he fell, and he hoped to be prepared for either outcome.

Queen Delany kissed her daughter's cheek goodbye, and took hold of Timothy's thick gloved hand. He turned to see Barbara's eyes beginning to spring up with tears.

"Be safe," he told her.

And Barbara, knowing she could not promise her own safety, and knowing there was now no privilege of safety left to Timothy, she said the only honest thing she could think to say.

"Just come back alive," she said.

The ringing drowned out all the war, and the light of their orb lifted, outshining the rain of fire boulders. And they shot out over the fields, grazing past the heads of giants, aiming northward at a lightning speed.

CHAPTER THIRTY-THREE
WHERE THEY WENT
✦

T hey came through the painting, a blinding flash of light in an otherwise black cavernous room, or, as their eyes adjusted, a room within a room. Queen Delany and Timothy had followed the globe, being reflected back into the window room that was now locked up inside Darius's underground laboratory dungeon, and within its cathedral-like ceilings the window room fit easily inside.

A noise, a jolt of electricity behind them, it crackled and moved to strike at Timothy in the back. Her Majesty's sword rang out from its sheath, crashing down upon Darius's cane before he could complete his work. In that instant, lightning bolts of electric current skipped up her sword, reaching her leather gloved hands. The Queen cried out in pain, but did not drop her sword, her gloves insulating most of the strike, so that it was only despicably agonizing, though not powerful enough to keep her from fighting back or to kill her.

By the blazing sparks that reflected in Darius's eyes, Timothy could see how furious that villain had been, that his ingenious weapon had been thwarted, that he could not easily win. He struck and struck again, each time the Queen slashed to deflect his attacks. Her form irregular and rough, with each new blow her hands seized tighter, her forearms stiffened and burned inside her muscles.

In the dark of that great room, Timothy brandished his sword that he'd been given while in Ismere. The scraping sound of the blade being lifted from its sheath alerted Darius to Timothy's intentions, and with a turn he jabbed the cane viciously into Timothy's chest, while at the same time Timothy struck a deep gash into Darius's right upper arm just below the shoulder.

By the force of the attack, and by virtue of its electrical power, Timothy was blasted backward through the air, smashing against a portion of the window room wall that still remained.

Yet, meanwhile, returning our story to the fields around the besieged city of Ismere: a sea of horsemen came flooding through the gate, fanning out their ranks to rush at full speed in a half-mooned shape toward their giant adversaries. Brave warriors dressed in their steel helmets and shimmering armor, and furs clasped upon some of their shoulders; Most rode with a javelin in one hand and the horse reins in the other, and with long tipped double-edged broadswords on their backs, or a bow and quiver strapped across their chest.

The thunder of thousands upon thousands of horse hoofs, and the battle cries of their riders, well armed with barbed arrows, or sword blades as finely sharpened as razors, but ahead of them a horde of giants, as tall as two-story buildings (and Atilion even taller). So that by comparison, these weapons of war seemed like children's toys in their hands.

Timothy coughed, trying to restart his lungs and breathing, that had suffered from Darius's electrified strike. His back aching and bruised from the force of his impact against the wall, and all the muscles in his chest felt like they had almost been wrenched in half.

And Delany had not fared so well either, for although she could unhand most of the kingdom's knights in combat, here there was an unfortunate difference. With every defensive movement, every swipe or thrust in Darius's direction, her hands and forearms burned more painfully. As planned, her gloves had done decently well at absorbing lightning shocks from the villain's cane, but they could not do enough. And with each new blow she grew weaker and less agile, until her swings became brutish, and desperate.

With a swift jab, Darius broke through her defenses, hitting with a full force into the Queen's thigh. She cried out in pain, toppling backward to the ground, at the base of Darius's towering wired tree-like mechanism. Sparks crawled up the trunk of the machine, singeing the ends of her hair.

From across the room there was a yell.

"I'll destroy it," Timothy threatened, standing over the globe with his sword drawn.

What this would mean, never having a way home, ruining all chances he'd ever have to see England again, to be reunited with his parents. And for what, the half-hearted chance that Darius might not kill them? But he had to try at least.

"You think I won't kill her, boy?" Darius sneered, then glanced again to the ground to see the Queen still writhing in pain from her wounds.

"No... but I think you can't kill her and save your globe, all at once," Timothy called out, his lungs still weakened, and his chest still struggling to gain breath.

"I'll make another," Darius answered him, but with the faintest shake in the timbre of his voice. "But in the interest of time, I shall, instead, make you an offer: Chop it to pieces, and I shall kill you both," and as Darius said this he was slowly taking steps toward the old window room, and Timothy, and the globe. "Or... spare it, and I will spare *your* life, and let you go home. Don't you want that?" he asked, using false tones of decency.

"You're lying," Timothy yelled, re-gripping his sword for a strike. Although he needn't have yelled, for Darius had already steadied closer to him, keeping his arms spread open as he walked, to make a show like he was not a threat.

"I am?" Darius responded. "How ever do you mean?"

"You can't build one, or else you would have done it

already... You need this, and I can take it away," Timothy said, reeling back for a final strike.

The sound of cane against a sword's blade, one metal scraping against another, and the audible crackling of electric bolts from the tip of Darius's weapon. In the last second, Timothy swung outward, instead of down at the globe, catching that old fiend completely by surprise.

But at once, Timothy's hands began to seize, clenching tighter and tighter, because of the shock. Soon his muscles would be useless, and so he knew he had to act quickly. With the flick of his wrist, he spun his blade around his enemy's weapon, as Asa had shown him during training (and as he'd spent a week's time practicing). The sharpened edge clinked and grinded, forcing both cane and sword down upon the face of the globe.

Like a battery instantly charged, or like the sound of a jet engine preparing for a blast, a high-pitched whirling noise started in the center of the globe and grew until it was deafeningly loud, almost immediately. Supercharged by Darius's electric cane, the globe became unstable. An otherworldly crystalline blue light emanated from its core; until, at last, it became far too much. An uncontrollable explosion shook through the room, a circular wall of tangible energy burst forth from the globe, blasting Timothy and Darius from their feet, and sending them hurtling through the air.

Timothy was thrown backward with an incredible force, smashing his back flatly into a stack of boxes and crates that shattered apart as he hit them, leaving scraps of wood collapsed down overtop of him.

Though Darius's was a worser fate (and, I should judge, that it was because his cane, that had been the initiator of this blast, in the instant the energy field exploded outward, an extra line of power was sent backward, up through his cane, dealing him with a double blow). The surge of immeasurable energy launched him across the length of that great room; and he hit with his back against the wired trunk of his towering machine. And like his own sparks had turned on him, they leapt from every limb and corner of that mechanism, as if to devour him.

And then there was a truly blinding flash of pure blue and vivid white shattering power, a force that split his machine in two, burying him beneath its rubble. And then the room was instantly and decidedly darkened, a sharp darkness in contrast to that unbearably blinding brilliant light.

CHAPTER THIRTY-FOUR
DISTANT STARLIGHT

✦

O nly a distant starlight came through the painting, in what had once been the window room, and the world in Gleomu was now darkened by night as well, and clouded on the mountain where Darius's prison estate stood, so that no other light could make its way through the holes in the high vaulted roof that had been torn open when Barbara and Timothy were first reflected back to Earth.

The great dungeon room was lightless and silent, until the unexpected voice of an elderly man broke through the stillness.

"Timothy!" his shaking voice rang out in the darkness. "Timothy! Answer now, won't you?"

"Wilbur?" asked a weakened voice, who was still collapsed on the stone floor, trying to regain her strength so that she might stand on her own.

And this voice, Queen Delany's voice, was exactly right. The surprising old man's voice was indeed that of Timothy's grandfather, Wilbur, who had spent the last seven or so hours diligently trying to remember things he'd very much so forgotten: Like how he had come to be in this strange house, and why he'd felt this incontrollable urge to eat, even though he did not feel truly hungry to begin with, and where his dear wife, Mattie, could have gone to (because he was almost very certain that she had been there in that odd house with him, although he had no means by which to prove this). And in this time he began to wonder how he had been stricken with a series of circularly formed burn marks, scattered across his back and front torso.

And it was not until after nightfall that he had remembered everything, especially the location of the secret doorway, and those steps leading down to the dungeon where Darius had held him prisoner for a considerable period of time, in order to run a litany of unsuccessful experiments on him.

But now, on this night, with a metal rod in his hand that he'd used to pry open the secret door, Wilbur, the King of Earth, came down the winded stairs, just in time to see his grandson and Darius blasted through the air, and then the blinding light of the explosion, followed by a blank blackness and all the room went dark. (Which, I should assume, would not be something one would hope to see, after being away from their life for a year's time, and after just so recently coming back to it.)

Wilbur followed the sound of the Queen's voice until he found her collapsed near the rubble of Darius's great machine.

"I think he's crashed into boxes... somewhere in that direction," Delany pointed vaguely, as Wilbur began to help her to her feet, which caused her to let out a short cry of pain, because her legs had been so wounded.

And with the Queen limping, using Wilbur's shoulder as a crutch, the two came fumbling in the dark to a heap of wooden crates, where they heard an almost inaudible low moaning, wedged beneath heavy pieces of timbered slat. They had found him, and it was something to be celebrated.

And yet, from Timothy's perspective his rescue went as so: In an almost pitch black room, he was startled back to his senses by a pressing immoveable weight, pinning his chest and legs, and arms, so that he could not budge the wood boards enough to free himself, and therefore he had come to the assumption that if unaided, he would eventually lose all strength to breathe, and be suffocated underneath this new trap.

Or after feeling a warm wetness trickling down his arm, he was forced to readjust his presumptions to include that he might, in fact, bleed to death before such a time.

Yet before he could come to terms with what that all meant, he heard a voice, muffled by the stack of loose wood now piled upon him, so that all he knew was that it was a man's voice, and nothing of who it might be, or what he might be saying. Leaving his only explanation to be: that this man's voice must be Darius's, and when he heard the short cry of a woman's voice, he had convinced himself that Darius, who must have revived himself, had gone back to finish his murder of the Queen, and that certainly he would be next in line, and helplessly stuck with no means of escape.

The weight of the crates upon his chest became less and less, until finally a man's hands began to reach at him in the almost completely darkened room. With his now free hands, Timothy pounded his fists at the man, desperately trying to save his own life, until he heard his grandfather's voice clearly.

"This is the thanks I get?" Wilbur slightly chuckled, in his own jolly way.

"Grandfather?" Timothy said, surprised and overjoyed that all seemed to be well again.

"You're safe, Tim," he answered, as his rounded and wrinkly stubby fingers reached around the boy, to embrace him and to lift him out of the pile.

Down charcoal hallways draped in the night of that place, they were eventually reunited with Matilde and Asa, although within their rejoicing there was also much concern. For Matilde, though she was still alive, she was hardly responsive, and Wilbur as a doctor of medicine by trade, said that she would by no means be able to survive very much longer without proper treatment from the palace physicians, who would be better equipped to handle the complications of her injuries, and Asa was also badly off, he had suffered severe burns and he had been dreadfully malnourished, but not in any life threatening way.

Yet he, unlike the Queen of Earth, was able to speak in hoarse whispers, and was quick to ask for food and water.

But still their predicament was clear, either they had to find a way to recalculate the globe in order to send themselves back to the palace, or else Matilde would not survive, maybe not even more than one day without proper treatment. This however, dear reader, is not the sort of easy thing you might imagine it to be.

For as it was, their globe, the one that was ripped away from the house in Mayfield, during the middle of the night, that was a globe from Earth, and therefore all the numbers and figures written within its almanac were transcribed in relation to Earth's position in the universe. Which, I trust, is an overly scientific way to say that it would not work in Gleomu, unless they were to figure out new numbers and settings for the globe.

And so, realizing this responsibility would fall to her as a veteran light traveler, Queen Delany, with the help of Wilbur and Timothy (after his arm had been bandaged), rushed through the house late that night in search of anything that might be used to measure the angles of stars. (Minding you that Matilde and Asa were first tucked soundly into warm beds, a comfort that would do little to aid Matilde, but one Asa had lacked for days, and was grateful for.)

And thankfully, not less than an hour later, they found locked up in the drawer of an upstairs study, just the device they had needed. Which if you fancy yourself a fan of either seamanship, or astronomy, then you might have heard of this device already; It was a sextant.

Howbeit, I do realize that that word will mean very little to a good number of people, and so, if you do not know how to image such a thing, it is a metal ringed instrument that works somewhat like the combination of a protractor and a telescope, and is used to measure

177

the angles of stars. Which in olden times was used to pinpoint a person's location on Earth, in relation to nearby stars, and usually within a range of accuracy of a few hundred yards, but that, of course, depended upon the skill of the measurer. Which fortunately for all involved, Delany was very good, after becoming tremendously better at science in her older years.

However, that night the bleakly cold northern mountains in Gleomu were heavily clouded, so that it took the Queen several hours, between passing clouds, to locate and measure the angles of common stars, like our own North Star[ψ]. It was a laborious and somewhat anticlimactic night, spent with mostly watching drifting clouds and the occasional glimmer of stars behind them. And those stars, Timothy watched for as long as he could from his stoop on the porch steps of the house, until he rested his head against an entry pillar and fell asleep, wrapped up warmly in a dense wool blanket.

But when the night was expired, and the sunlight broke over the ridge of that shallow mountain valley, by then, Delany had finished her recalculations, and once again the world and cities of Gleomu shone out of the

---

ψ Which is named Polaris on Earth, but in Gleomu they call it Eard, and there it is not used in any form for navigation, like we would use it on Earth, but is simply a very bright and beautiful star. And as chance would have it, at this time of the year it could be seen both from on Earth and in Gleomu; Which if you stop to consider that fact, is really such a miracle, for Matilde's sake, and I'm convinced is the only way that she stood any chance at all for survival.

painting, that still hung, somewhat precariously, on the wall of the broken and stolen window room, locked up inside Darius's underground dungeon.

And from out of the painting, as he came closer to have a better look, Timothy saw the capitol city, Ismere, still surrounded by a giant's army, and with the fires from their catapults burning in every district. It did not appear to be the safest place they could have chosen to run to for help.

"I should go first," Wilbur spoke up, also seeing the images from the city. "I'm the only one who isn't wounded-"

"Even so, I cannot join you," Asa interrupted, which was unlike his character to do, but it seemed these thoughts had been weighing on him for some time by then, perhaps since they had first begun to recalculate the globe. "The King forbids it," he ended with.

"What if we said we forced you?" Timothy answered quickly, but then knew by everyone's harsh gazes that he had crossed some sort of a boundary line, and that he should have known better.

"Timothy..." Asa shook his head disapprovingly. "Then I would forbid myself from it."

And after this Wilbur continued on, to explain his idea that they could travel by note to the city (exactly like Timothy and Barbara had done previously, when they had sent letters back and forth between the palace and Matilde's regiment of soldiers, at the start of their journeys). Except that in Wilbur's plan, he would touch the paper note to the globe, thereby using it to travel to the city, and after a few minutes the paper would return to the window room, with a message letting them know if it was safe for travel.

And this of course was a marvelous idea, and a few moments later the globe was charged and the light was ready, and Wilbur, the King of Earth, was whisked away, through the painting, across the land of Gleomu. And, as they had hoped, a few minutes later a crinkled note floated down at their feet with one large hand-scribbled word at the top of the page.

"**SAFE**"

And likewise, after seeing that good news, Delany carried a wounded Matilde up with her in the orb, because the old woman was too frail to make the trip on her own, leaving Timothy and Asa alone to watch the siege of Ismere unfold before their eyes, as images of the battle and the burning city still came through one of the corner vignettes of the painting like a moving picture. Nothing was said until the note returned, "**Safe**" written below the other inscription.

"I'll come back..." Timothy said, after touching the paper to the globe, "to bring you supplies, and news about the war."

"That is kind of you, young prince," Asa answered, as he nodded a "thank you", stepping back from the globe as light began to form around Timothy and the letter.

"When should I expect you?" Asa shouted, because the noise of the globe was now very loud.

"Tomorrow," Timothy shouted in return, or so was his plan when he reset the time on the globe for one day, precisely. However, a lot can happen within the course of a day, as Timothy would soon find, a lot indeed.

CHAPTER THIRTY-FIVE

THE GARDENS

"T im, you're alive!" Barbara said, as she threw her arms around him.

Perhaps just as excited, and we shouldn't fault her for this, that she'd still had a friend with her to help her through the war, as she was that this particular friend had fared as well as he had.

"Ow! A little less, please," Timothy said wincing. "My arm's not so good," he continued, until Barbara had noticed his fresh bandage on the upper portion of his right arm, and with that she quickly apologized, coming back to her normal self again.

That morning Timothy's orb had landed in the palace gardens, near the fountain where they'd first met King Corwan and Queen Delany some weeks prior, during the King's birthday celebration. But this time the gardens were all but emptied, with every available palace guard, gardener, and butler sent to take a watch along the city walls. The stunning gardens, with its well trimmed lawn and hedges, were eerily silent, except for the trickle of water flowing from off the marble fountain.

"How is it here?"

Timothy could see the city, and the fires, and the destruction during his descent in the orb, and so he did not exactly care for an account of the war. Howbeit, Barbara knew what he'd meant, and so she answered, "Your grandmother and the Queen were carried off by the palace physicians... They say there's good hope." Barbara said this truthfully, but she could see the doubt in his eyes, and so she added, "And... I'm sure they meant it."

There was a moment of pause.

"And what about Asa?" Barbara asked, her eyes were regretful and face saddened, like she'd expected to hear the worst sort of news. "Is he not coming?"

"No, he's not... and he won't be," Timothy answered, with a somber expression on his face, taking a seat on the edge of the fountain.

At that news, Barbara nearly collapsed down beside him, looking like she was about to cry giant tears into the palms of her hands, which finally made Timothy realize how his words had sounded.

"Oh. No, no... he's not dead," Timothy insisted, trying to make things better, shaking her arm softly so that she'd look at him, but sadly her face was already wet with tears. "It's just, he can't come back... he's not allowed to. It's the King's orders, remember, 'no native born person can use light travel.' That's all."

"Well it's still awful," Barbara answered in full sobs, wiping her tears with the back of her hand. (It's not that this news was all that bad, considering the alternatives, but I believe, it's just that Barbara, who was not so used to crying, could not turn her tears off so easily, after she had already made up her mind to start.)

"So... he's stuck there, then?" she finally managed to say, after a little more sniffling, and once she had thoroughly died her eyes.

"Looks that way..." he answered.

Timothy sighed a little, and used his hands to prop himself up as they sat staring out over such an immaculate garden; Perfect plants and hedges, and stone statues, in the center of a burning city at war, with waning hopes for victory.

After another pause, that seemed to go on forever, Timothy finally spoke again, a question that neither knew the answer to, "Do you think the King would change his mind?"

CHAPTER THIRTY-SIX

OF KINGS

✦

During that day, Timothy and Barbara went to check on his grandmother, who'd received some sort of medication, and various herbal salves, and was at that time asleep in her room, the one that had been set aside for her during visits.

When they'd arrived, they saw seated in a chair at one side of the bed was Timothy's grandfather, who sat cupping Matilde's hand, and every so often he would brush the hairs from her face, as he had done nearly since she'd arrived, and had not left her bedside.

And on the other side of the bed stood one of the palace physician, the head physician in fact (whose name was Dorton, and who had been good friends with Wilbur and Matilde for many years). He said that she, "...had shown signs of improvement, and would be better than her old self in days." Which was perhaps a bit of positive thinking, but they thought it was good to know at least that she would be alright.

And for a good portion of the morning they pulled up chairs to the bedside, to watch for any improvements, and to listen to the men as they discussed possible methods of treatment, and the condition of Matilde's recovery, but all in the ways that trained doctors would speak. Some of which, that at either times, Timothy or else Barbara would vaguely comprehend, but most of it was well beyond their current educations. And even during Wilbur's lengthy explanations (whenever they'd thought to ask a question), even that was not always understood, so that they eventually learned to stop asking those types of questions, in favor of other ones that they might better understand.

Including a question that Timothy had wondered for some time about:

During a long break in the conversation, Timothy leaned over to his grandfather to ask, what he thought might be a private question.

"Why do they call you a king, grandfather? I mean... you're not one, you know, not really." And Barbara had leaned in, as well, to hear the answer to Timothy's question, being quite curious herself.

"I'm not?" the old man chuckled, in his jolly way.

Timothy and Barbara exchanged glances, as if they had missed something.

"Oh, there's no need to whisper, my boy. Everyone here knows we're just regular folks on Earth," he smiled.

"But why-" Barbara began to ask, but she was cut off.

"Oh, it was King Corwan's idea," Wilbur said, almost brushing them off. "He said he didn't want there to be any formality between friends, and so he made your grandmother a queen, and once we got married, well that made me a king, I suppose."

"And no one cares you're not really King?" Barbara asked.

Wilbur sat back in his chair like he was thinking. "In practice, I'd say, most people have forgotten all about it, or else, no," he said answering Barbara's question. "I don't think they care... Which was maybe Corwan's point in this whole thing."

And that seemed to make enough sense to them, however Wilbur did not appear to be finished with his point.

He spoke again, raising his finger like he were to ask them something important. "How did Elizabeth get to be Queen in England?" he asked.

Timothy scratched the side of his chin, trying to recall what he'd learned in civics class, from last quarter.

"She was born into it, right?" Wilbur said after a brief second, answering his own question.

"Yes," and "I guess so," they replied.

"Well, there you have it," Wilbur said, as if that had settled it. "You see, your grandmother," he said, pointing toward Matilde, "she was born to be the Queen of Earth. And so whether or not they know it back home, we only try to do what's best for our people... Meaning, we don't need fancy palaces and servants to prove it, we can be real kings and queens, even if we're fake ones."

In the afternoon, Timothy and Barbara were treated to a small supper of toasted grain bread, and olive paste, topped with tomato, and served with a ruby colored vinegar dipping oil, and there was a small glass of wine for each of them.

And eventually, when the day had waned on and it was nearly sunset, and they had grown tired of waiting, Timothy began to ask around, wondering when the King would return to the palace for the evening. Though apparently that as the wrong sort of question, for no one expected the King to return at all, until the war had ended. And lastly, there was information from one of the attendants in the palace (an old woman who'd been a nurse to the King's grandfather), she said that she'd heard from others, that King Corwan had taken a post by the break in the wall, and that he would be there for most of the night.

Which left him with no other choice (if Timothy had wanted to speak to the King about Asa's return), except for him to make his way out from the palace gate, through the cindered and charred parts of the city at sunset. And after a long walk, as the last rays faded from view, the Prince of Earth found the King of Gleomu standing watch at a gaping hole in the wall, which had grown slightly larger since he'd last left. King Corwan stood on top of the broken pieces of the wall, with his long sword drawn in front of him, the tip of it pointed to the ground, and he had his hands resting on the hilt of it, like a regal guard.

"Excuse me, Your Majesty," Timothy said, after clambering up the mound of broken wall to stand beside the King.

Corwan lowered his gaze for only a brief second to see who stood beside him, before returning his attention again to the giant's army encamped in the fields around the city.

"Good," the King said. "I was hoping you would come."

"You were?" Timothy asked, as all the sunlight was at last fallen to the west of them, and the soldiers at their stations began to light the torch lamps.

"Of course," the King said proudly. "I've heard what happened with Darius, and how you'd saved my Queen's life." And for a longer moment, Corwan took his eyes off the battle entirely, and with an expression of tenderness Timothy had only seen equaled by his own father, the King said, "All my thanks to you, Prince. I am forever grateful."

And then setting his attentions forward once more, he continued, "When this is all over, we shall have a feast in your honor." The King smiled at the thought of a grand feast, but for now there was still the war to be had, so that the expression of battle never truly left his face, even as he said this.

And they both went on again, to watch the giant's army for any signs of movement, or attack, but there was none of that.

After a few minutes, Timothy saw over his shoulder, other watchmen making their way between posts, and he heard the clinking of metal as supply men delivered extra stocks of arrows, and spears for the artillery. Yet, besides this, the city was quiet, and Timothy had finally got the courage to ask what he'd come for.

"Your Majesty... I came to ask about Asa," Timothy managed to say.

"Did you now?"

By the deepness of the King's voice, it made Timothy instantly feel as if he were not going to get a positive answer, but since he'd already begun the process of asking, he thought he might as well finish. After all, the King was "forever grateful" to him, as he had said, perhaps this gratitude might extend to other areas as well.

"You see, he's stuck in the north, and he... he can't come back because of your laws. Though, if you'd allow me, I could bring him back by morning."

Even saying these words Timothy felt foolish, and like he had overstepped his bounds to even ask King Corwan to make this exception in his laws, and he felt sure the King would be furious with him; Although he was not, not even slightly.

"And why should I change them?" Corwan asked, with his hands still resting on the handle of his royal sword, shoulders back and arms straight, with his eyes closely fixed on his duty as a watchman.

Timothy thought it obvious. "Because he's your son," he answered.

"Timothy," the King spoke, like he would explain something important, and he looked at the boy in the eyes as he said it. "If he were myself, I would not change the laws... That machine is a weapon, and the less we use of it the better."

Timothy's face was distraught as he thought about the King's words for a moment, and then pointing out across the plains toward the giant's army, he said, "Then if it is a weapon, why not use it? Send out an army to attack them from behind, or something... we can win the battle, Your Majesty, there's still time."

By then the night had fully fallen on the city, and the flickering torchlight cast deep shadows on the King's face and beard.

"Young man, don't you remember... Darius would have used that machine for great evil, not just in our world, but in all worlds."

And as they stood there a tiny piece of the wall, that had not yet fallen, finally broke loose and fell, clicking against the larger stone slabs as it skipped down the face of the pile on which they stood, and it landed with an almost silent thud on the dirt outside the city wall.

"But you're not Darius, Your Majesty," Timothy eventually spoke, after searching through his mind for something that seemed right to say. "Surely, you would use the globe for good."

The King breathed in a deep breath, as he answered.

"Yes, I'm sure that I would... But we do well to withhold such great power, even from ourselves."

"But why?" Timothy asked, with the glow of lit torches, and the light of stars and the moon shining down upon them.

"Because I shall not always be king," Corwan answered.

CHAPTER THIRTY-SEVEN

THE PALACE

W hen Timothy returned to the palace that night. There was a commotion in the halls, and an obvious unsettledness, and he was sure he'd thought he heard someone crying. In fact, he'd nearly stopped one of the waiters by the kitchen door to ask what had been the matter, that was until he saw Barbara leaving the dining hall. She too had been recently tearful, and her face seemed to be saddened for sometime.

"What's going on here?" Timothy asked her, while still glancing around at some of the other passersby leaving the dining hall, who'd seemed to be equally as sad.

Barbara's expression was mournful, and she spoke softly in a whisper.

"The King's son has just died," she answered.

"Who, Asa?" Timothy asked, but realizing as he said this, that that was not a very thought out response.

Barbara's eyes fluttered, as if she'd been slightly startled, slightly amused by Timothy's lack of deduction at the moment.

"What? Of course not, don't be silly. How could we even know that anyway?" she answered. "No, it's one of his younger son's, Tahan," she said, stepping out from the middle of the hallway, so that she would not be rudely in peoples' way as they spoke.

"It was during the horsemen's attack," she began to explain, " ...when you left to fight Darius. Both he and his horse were knocked off their feet by Atilion's giant club, and he's just died an hour ago." And Barbara stopped to wipe a bit of moistness from under her eyelid. "In fact, a lot of the soldiers died in the attack," she continued.

And then looking back toward the open doors leading to the dining hall, she said, "And I overheard a woman at dinner, who'd said that she'd heard from one of the generals' wives, that the walls won't last another day of this, and they say then that the giants will just wait us out, and walk in one night when we least expect it, and when our supplies have run low."

"Seems hopeless, doesn't it?" she ended with.

"Yeah," was all Timothy could think to reply, overwhelmed by this flood of awful news.

A young woman and a man, who'd wore the same sort of physician's clothes as they'd seen earlier, walked by, and the two'd stopped talking, until the man and woman had gone by them.

"Is Asa still not coming back?" Barbara asked, once she and Timothy had their privacy again.

"No, the King won't allow it," he answered.

And following this, Timothy, who was by now quite thirsty, and with his stomach growling from his long walks, both to and from the North Gate, and from not having a full meal previously, he took some leftover tea and crackers from the dining hall, and they continued to speak for hours in one of the common sitting rooms:

about the war, about what would happen to them if they had to flee the city, and if they would be back in time for the end of what would have been our summer here on Earth, or, if not, would people say they had died as well.

Yet throughout the night, though, neither of them wanted to speak about the very real inevitable possibility that either of them might actually die during the war, and so they spoke of it only as a hypothetical, and not for very long.

And when they had finished, as they were returning to their own quarters, and while the steps of their feet echoed in the late night hours, through the empty marble palace halls, Timothy said these words:

"You know, *we* can go back home, when this is all done... and the people there may have thought we'd been dead, but we wouldn't have been. And we can go back to how things were, but they can't. If this city and the palace are destroyed: then Asa, and Delany, and Corwan, and everyone else, they lose their homes, and they can't travel to another world to forget about it."

" ...Or they're not allowed to," Barbara added.

"Right," Timothy said, agreeing.

It was late after midnight, and Timothy lay awake on his bed, with his other new sword propped up against the pillow beside him, and he'd had the note folded inside his pocket, in case he'd overslept. But even as he lay there, he could not help but think, that the city would be doomed if they could not find a way to stop Atilion and his evil army.

And it was sometime during that night of tossing and turning, though it was hard to say exactly when, while laying upon his comfortable bed, that Timothy had had a very selfless thought, perhaps an evidence that he had grown somewhat during his journeys, thus far.

There was a way to stop Atilion, to disrupt his army, maybe enough so that they could win, and he was the only one that could do it. But he would need to first borrow something from Barbara, without her knowing.

CHAPTER THIRTY-EIGHT

THE CHALLENGE

By the first light of morning, Timothy was awake. By then, he had, with the help of one of the palace maids, gathered an extra change of clothes for Asa, and some medicine, and all the food he could fit inside a pack, and he stood alone in the palace gardens at sunrise. In one hand, he held the scribbled note that would carry him along, back to the broken window room, and in the other was Barbara's crossbow, the one that was a present to her from Queen Delany, and he had meant to borrow it indefinitely, and he hoped she would not be angry with him.

Light stretched over the eastern garden walls. The note began to glow in his hand, of its own accord, and the shrill ringing noise began again. Then, like a lightning bolt, he was swept away once more, reflected back to the broken window room, for what perhaps would be his last time.

Flashing through the painting and back into Darius's poorly lit underground basement, Timothy set the pack of things he'd brought for Asa against a half-wall in the window room. He charged the globe and set the point of Barbara's arrow at an exact place, a place that he'd well decided on the night before. The arrow began to emit a golden light of its own.

There was a noise of someone at the basement stairs.

"Forgot to say goodbye, did you?" Asa said jokingly. He stood at the base of the stairs, and was leaning most of his weight onto a homemade crutch he'd fashioned to help him around that massive lonely house, until his legs had healed entirely.

Timothy turned, and very solemnly replied, "Goodbye, Asa."

At once, a look of terror spread across the wounded prince's face, he knew that tone, and how Timothy had meant it.

"No!" he shouted, but it was too late.

In a moment, the arrow, and the crossbow, and Timothy, were lifted into the air, and shot through the painting, and across the northern country, back to the place where Timothy had chosen.

It was still early morning, as Timothy passed through the open fields, letting the high grass sink around his ankles. Behind him, in one of the few standing watchtowers along the wall, a warning bell rang, and he heard the noise of a horn being blown to call soldiers to action. But still he kept walking, evenly paced, he had ten minutes left and did not want to waste it rushing.

Not very far ahead of him, Timothy saw the catapults, as big as houses. And even before he was close enough to have a look at them, the disgusting stench of giants floated in the air, seeping into his nose. (And so that you can imagine it, commonly most giants stink of rotten meat and the foulest body odors.) In his ears were their snorings, until he came closer.

Thud. Thud.

As he drew nearer, one of the sentry giants noticed him and beat the warning drum to wake the rest of the army. Within seconds, he heard foul-odored giants calling between themselves: "Well look at that", "Just a child" some would say, or either they would erupt in an arrogant laughter.

Finally, when he'd come to a reasonable stopping distance Timothy cupped his hands to his mouth and shouted, "I've come to challenge Atilion."

But this had caused an even greater roar of laughter, which came to rest with Atilion's own treacherous and stony laughter. The mountainous giant pushed through the crowd and stood in front of his army, gazing down at his new adversary.

"You want a challenge, little boy?" he laughed, and his other giants laughed, shaking the ground beneath Timothy's feet.

Timothy pretended not to be afraid (and did a good job at it), but his stomach churned with every word.

"We can settle this war now," he shouted, as bravely as he could. "If I kill you, your army has to leave."

Atilion sneered and grinned as he spoke. "Do they? And what do I get in return, when I kill you... your surrender?" he asked, waving his deadly club at the city.

Timothy paused to answer this, and after looking around at the deformed giants' faces, and at the ominous catapults all around him, he said loudly, "Well, no... You would kill us anyway, but this just gives us a fair chance."

The giants, of course, thought this was all devilishly funny, so that Atilion had to yell insults at them so that they would be silent.

"Alright, little child," the giant lord answered. And then giving a wicked grin, "I will play your game."

Wind swept past the grass and Timothy's pant legs, as Atilion drew back his spiked club, the size of a massive ancient fallen oak tree. Timothy raised up his crossbow, hoping that the ringing would have started by now, but there was nothing. He gave himself too much time, he thought.

Atilion paused at the top of his strike. "Have you only got *one* arrow?" he chuckled, and chided the boy.

"That's all I need," Timothy answered, in his full voice.

However, Atilion, not wanting to make this challenge appear too easy for himself, and turning back to judge the expressions on his men's faces, he decided to draw this out, so to not lose the fear and respect of his army.

Yet, even at this same time there was another thing that had happened, the horn that had blown some minutes ago within the city had served as a message to call all the remaining horsemen to battle. And a charge had begun, at full speed, a formation of warhorses led by King Corwan himself.

And still, even while seeing the cavalry horses of Ismere approaching at a blinding speed, Atilion arrogantly yelled, loudly, so that he would not go unheard, "Fine. Let it not be said that I did not give you your 'fair chance,' " he besmirched, wide and horrid.

"Take your shot, infant child," the giant warlord shouted, spreading his arms at length apart, still holding the club, outstretched in his fist.

"*Finally!*" Timothy shouted within his head.

The ringing began to whirl inside his ears. He lifted up his crossbow, aiming the tip of the arrow at Atilion's face. The ringing built louder, but was instantly silenced, as soon as the arrow released from the bow.

It sailed upward through the air, straight toward the giant's eye, but in the last second Atilion swung his club as a shield, and the arrow sunk deep into the wood.

Almost immediately, the giant king became disoriented. He tried to wield his club, striking Timothy down in his rage, but the arrow and the club lifted high above the battlefield, out of reach. While at the same time, King Corwan, galloping at full speed, his armor and his horse's armor glimmering in the morning sunlight. Wrapping the reins in his hand, he drew himself up, so that he was standing upon the horse's saddle as he rode, unstoppably, toward Atilion and his murderous army.

And with one hand bound in the reins, and another holding fast to a mighty javelin, that in itself may have been twice the King's own size, Corwan dug the toe of his boot under the pommel of his horse's saddle to support his stance, and he flung that javelin with all the force and strength that his body could possess, and it struck the giant, Atilion, who fell down dead upon the field like a thunder clap.

To the sound of Atilion's fall, his giant army turned to flee, leaving behind them: giant swords, and weapons, and artillery. And from that day hence, there has not a giant dared to set foot in the land of Gleomu, nor to cross the northern borders, except to bring their yearly gifts to present before the King, as were the terms of their surrender.

CHAPTER THIRTY-NINE

SPRINGTIME

I n the late springtime, when the weather was more
forbearing, and safe travels could be made, and
once the breaks in the wall had been mended, and the
citizens of Ismere had begun to join together to restore
some of what the giants' fire boulders had burned, or
decimated. It was at that time that a rescue team was
appointed to retrieve the Prince, Asa, from his
"imprisonment" in Darius's house.

Through much better conditions than their previous
ventures had shown them, they rode across the plains
through the pass, and onward to the high plains, with
clear sun and the sweet smell of spring flowers, to
Hrim, and upward along the mountain trail to Darius's
english-style house, hidden within the shallow
mountain valley.

Among this group that made the journey, there were
only allowed those men who'd first volunteered with
Matilde at the beginning (and only those of them who'd
been brave enough to make the full journey). There
being: King Corwan, and Prince Reuel, and the fourteen
remaining men who'd survived the giant war, and
Wilbur and Matilde, and Timothy and Barbara, of
course, because they were the only two of them who'd
known the way.

And there in the house they found Asa, rested and thoroughly recovered; Although several pounds heavier, after staving off his boredom and the winter months, eating platefuls of perfect food from Darius's kitchen. And as with others, his memory had taken a similar affect, although not nearly as drastic, so that within no time he was relaying to them the stories of his confinement, and about all of what he'd read within Darius's scientific books, and about the glory of making instant food, purely by molecular compound. Except that some of what he'd said made those from Earth, especially Wilbur and Matilde, laugh aloud though they tried to restrain themselves, because they understood he did not fully realize all that he was describing, as someone from Earth might.

Saying things like: "Automobiles are fueled with olive oil," or comparing train engines to lifeless metal land dragons, that blow smoke from their spouts and can transport men several hundred miles at a time.

Notwithstanding, as a true budding scientist, during his time there he'd made several substantial, or noteworthy, discoveries and observations.

And they, in the order he told about them, were these:

Firstly, that when Atilion's club and Timothy's arrow had been shot away from the battlefield, and squeezed through the painting, that monstrous club had smashed apart the globe and had fallen backward, tearing the painting through the center. And it was Asa's newly formed scientific opinion that the globe and the painting could never be repaired. (And this summation was in fact true. After all, at the time of their creations, both the globe and the painting had been made by far better sciences, and were far more intricately designed than any of them would ever be capable, within their lifetimes, of achieving. Those precious artifacts were gone for good, along with all the abilities they'd possessed, and there was no hope that they would ever be put back together.)

And secondly, Timothy's "compass", that he had brought with them to Gleomu when they'd first arrived, well it was not in fact a compass at all, as you might have guessed. Though, as Asa had decided, it was most likely a gauge of some kind, which is another thing he had read about in Darius's science books. (This, again, was correct; To be specific, this device that Timothy had brought along with them under the assumption of a compass was actually a luminometer, or a gauge that measures trace amounts of light energy.)

And thirdly, and this was saved for the end, because Asa had been so excited about it: In his exploration of the grounds of the house, he'd stumbled upon a flying machine, laid under a thick sheet cover, and stored within a shed adjacent to the house.

It was just like the drawing Barbara had seen sketched out in Darius's study, months before. It was all earthy brown with canvas propellors, and a wind sail along its ridge. A perfect flying machine, except that there was a small tear in the sail, and *that* would need to be mended before any test flight could be had.

Though happily, the job of this, by their own design, was quickly taken up by Wilbur and Asa, who spent a week's time combing through every inch of the machine's surface, polishing cables, and triple checking rudders, until they understood its mechanics completely, and the entire thing was marvelous to look at.

However, when the search party's rations began to dwindle, to levels needed for a safe return trip home, King Corwan made plans to leave there, for fear that they might become tempted to eat Darius's food, and would soon begin to forget themselves, as all who'd eaten that food before them had done.

And on the following day, the team made preparations to leave, but Wilbur and Asa had hoped to take their flying machine back with them to Ismere, and also Timothy and Barbara could not wait to try it out, leaving one space open for Matilde, if she would squeeze into it.

"Please come," Wilbur said to her that morning, as they wheeled their spectacular flying machine out of the shed and onto the lawn in front of the house.

But Matilde, who'd been deathly afraid of planes for years by that point, shook her head and her long grey streaked hair, and answered him, "You know I can't."

To this the old man looked at his wife, and ducking under the wing, came to her and put his arm around her shoulder. And they both stood there, side-by-side, admiring that elegant machine.

And after a moment had passed, Wilbur, the King of Earth, pointed at his work.

"Just look at it," he said. "Tell me it's not beautiful."

"It's not beautiful," the old woman muttered.

Wilbur chuckled in his jolly way.

"Come on, now... if you weren't afraid of planes, wouldn't that be the sort you'd like to fly in?" he asked, giving her a tender squeeze with his arm.

Matilde drew her fingers through her hair and gave that machine a hard look.

"Probably..." she finally answered.

"See there," Wilbur said looking at his Queen. "How about, starting now, you're only afraid of all other planes, except this one?"

"Now you're just being silly," she replied.

"Oh, come on," Wilbur insisted. "We've only got so much time left, to do the things we want."

"If we go up in that thing, for sure," Matilde snapped back, showing her wit, and the two began to laugh at each other's reactions, and eventually, Matilde decided to make an exception, just this once.

And it is my opinion that she could not have been happier, as their sail caught the wind, and they all flew up above the crest of the valley, seeing miles and miles of the land of Gleomu stretched out before them, waving farewell to King Corwan and the rest below them, pointed onward to Ismere, their new home; A city of safety and prosperity, and new kinships... and if all their world back on Earth had thought that they had died, and had grieved them, at least they would know the truth of it, if only they and no others, that they were very much alive.

AFTERWORD

A year, with its seasons, had come and gone in that world: There was the marriage of Pemberley, the Queen's youngest daughter. And as for Timothy, he had vastly improved upon his knack for swordsmanship, and had also grown rather keen to matters of the council, so that Wilbur said that he should make a fine court questioner one day, if the laws allowed for a foreigner to sit at court.

And during that time, Barbara had not been idle either. Among other things, she would take long walks with the Queen, who seemed to fancy her, through the countryside, and she had grown to be the life at royal parties, and gatherings. So that she had many suiters requesting if she could be betrothed, but to that Matilde, the Queen of Earth, who'd taken Barbara in as almost a second daughter, always had a standard reply. That, " ...she [Barbara] was too young for that now, but when she was ready she would make the decision on her own."

It was a year of all the best that Gleomu had to offer, and in the fall, when the last brick of the last building in Ismere had been rebuilt, King Corwan, who was true to his word, held a feast in Timothy's honor: Three days of banquets, and dancing, and performers reenacting scenes from the Great Giant War, as they had come to call it.

Yet, as delightful as it may have been, a year had come and gone, and Timothy and Barbara, Wilbur and Matilde had decided to ride out to Lochshire for May Festival, and on their return they had elected to take a detour, along the rim of a gully river with steep canyon walls on either side, and a stream that poured over waterfalls and splashed in deep pools below.

The ride was pleasant enough, but they had been traveling all day long, and Timothy was by then very bored. So he began to fiddle with his gauge that he had brought along with them just in case, as it had become his habit to do if they were planned to travel to someplace new. Most often, this habit would only disappoint him, however this time was quite different.

When they rounded a bend in the river, the needle on the center dial began to spike. Timothy could not withhold his excitement.

"I found something," he shouted to the others ahead of him, and leapt off his horse, following the direction of the mysterious reading, or signal, of some sort. Which led him at a brisk pace through the treeline, and down a narrow, almost unnoticeable footpath to the bottom of the canyon: The needle on his gauge slowly rising as he descend further toward the stream.

At last he was stopped in front of a waterfall, cascading over a giant single boulder, as tall as the walls of Ismere itself, and the waterfall fell into a deep circular pool.

"Have you lost your head, Tim?" Barbara shouted, trying to keep her footing as she followed down the narrow pathway, holding up the hem of her dress so she would not trip.

And when she at last made it safely to the bottom, in front of the waterfall, they heard yelling from the canyon ledge above them.

"What's going on you two?" Matilde yelled down below.

But before Timothy could answer for himself, Barbara turned around quickly, shouting, "Your grandson's gone mad, my lady." Barbara turned back to Timothy, still smiling at her wit.

"I am not," he said to her. "Here, hold this." And he gave her his gauge for safe keeping, and began to unstrap his boots.

Whatever his gauge had found, it must be behind that rock, Timothy thought, and he was sure of it.

With his shoes off, Timothy dove into the water.

"What? Are we swimming now?" Wilbur said, having just caught up with Matilde, at the brim of the canyon.

"Apparently," Barbara yelled as an answer.

The water crashed over his head with a beating weight, even in late spring it was icy cold. Timothy took in a deep breath, and dove as far as his lungs would take him.

"There's a cave," he yelled, coming back up for air, but the pounding waterfall drowned away his words.

"What?" Barbara shouted, trying to be heard above the crashing water, but it was too late, Timothy had disappeared below the surface again.

Kicking and pushing himself beneath the current, Timothy pulled through the underwater cave. Faintly seen through the murky water ahead of him, a pale airy greenish light, there was a single beam through the water, and he followed that light, almost sure he would drown. Until he came to the surface of a glass still pool, in an underground cave.

Bulbous columns of stone grew down from the ceiling, and a slant ray of light beamed through a small opening in the roof. Climbing out at the edge of the pool, dripping wet hair and clothes, Timothy saw on the walls of the cavern room surrounding him, cave drawings and paintings, but not rudimentary paintings, great works of art, depicting some moments in histories long forgotten. And surrounding each painting, walls and walls of text, in a writing he could not then understand.

And then, it caught his eye. There, directly across from the ancient pool, now illuminated by the single shaft of light descending from the ceiling was a globe: a real globe, a light globe, nearly the same in every way as the one they had before. He had found it, Timothy had found a way home.

Throwing up his hands, water dripping off his shirt and pooling around his shoeless feet, he screamed, a shout of victory, of triumph.

"Woo!!" he shouted from deep within his lungs, and the echo of it repeated off the cavern walls.

CPSIA information can be obtained at www.ICGtesting.com
Printed in the USA
LVOW11s0146311214

420938LV00001BA/131/P